NO SUCH QUEEN

Blurb

Atticus DuPont is my stalker.
My savior.
My captor.
He wants to keep me for himself.

Just as I started to trust August, I was yanked from his arms and thrown into the deadly underbelly of the criminal kingdom. Atticus is my only ally in this place, and he revels in knowing that I must rely on him if I want to survive—if I want to get back to August.

Atticus is dangerous, and I don't trust him.
I despise him.
I ache for him.

But the playboy billionaire has demons of his own. Somehow, I started to fall for him. And I can't leave now.

Mighty is the sword.
Violent are the Crown's enemies.

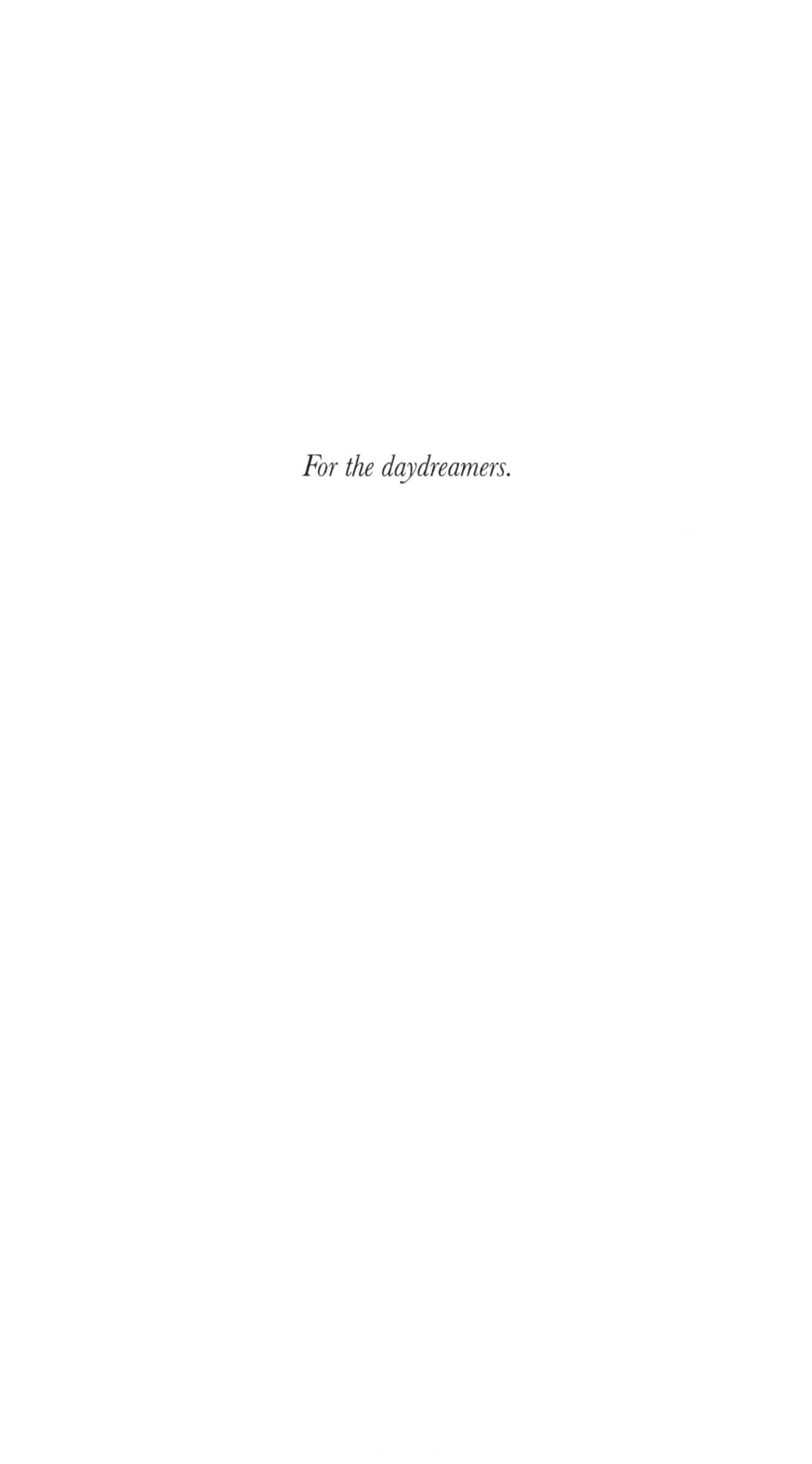

For the daydreamers.

Chapter One

"There is a full lockdown in effect, sir. There is no entry or exit from the castle," said the guard at the gate. He was an arrogant man with a thin mustache and a puffed up chest. His position as the gatekeeper for the royal family probably made him feel important, and he probably fucked his wife every Saturday in the missionary position. He had a scuffed up wedding band on his left hand and the look of a man who didn't know good sex even though there was plenty of porn to study. The Mrs. probably laid there like a dead fish, praying he'd hurry up and come so she could go back to reading her romance novels and flick her own clit.

The guard probably had never seen a man die.

Probably had never *killed* a man.

But here he was, telling me I couldn't enter the castle's gates. As if he were important enough to stop me.

Every second he kept me from getting inside, my anger grew. I'd been eager to spill some blood. Hell, it wouldn't take much convincing for me to drive a knife in his neck.

A palm slapped my passenger window, but I didn't flinch.

I never flinched.

There was a sea of paparazzi encircling my car, trying to catch a glimpse of something intriguing for their exclusive news report. It was nearly impossible to hear anything over the roar of their questions.

My lungs were filled with the stench of death, and the air was filled with a thick layer of smoke. Several hours were spent extinguishing the flames that had engulfed the royal ballroom. In the midst of the fire, the castle was half burned to the ground.

"Do you know who I am?" I asked, lowering my sunglasses with my bandaged hand. I peered at him with dark eyes, boring all my annoyance right down to his very pathetic soul. "My name is Atticus DuPont. King Augustus summoned me. I am Lady Abernathy's last contact, and he has questions." I had a series of missed calls and frantic texts from Augustus, Adonis, and a few royal advisors, each one becoming more urgent as they progressed.

The older guard widened his eyes. I was irritated when people failed to recognize me. It was not because I was an egotistical asshole, but because it made my job more difficult. I found life to be much easier when the majority of the population feared me. My name had power, and I worked damn hard for it.

The guard's sputtering response was satisfying. "Of course, Mr. DuPont. I'll open the gate. His Highness is at the explosion site near the ballroom entrance."

My car slowly moved through the driveway, and the thick crowd of paparazzi pressed against the gate. Some thrust their expensive cameras through the bars. They wanted a picture of the burned castle. Or better yet—a snapshot of their grieving king. A few tears could earn them *millions*. The police did a wretched job of keeping the nosy intruders at bay.

Many of them shouted questions as I crossed the threshold.

"Is it true Lady Abernathy is dead?"

"Can you confirm that King Augustus is in the ICU?"

"Do you have any leads on who attacked the Crown?"

As I rolled up my window, a few of them snapped

photos. I schooled my expression into a mixture of panicked concern and agony. My world was a stage and I had to put on the best performance of my life.

Christine depended on it.

I weaved through the parade of fire trucks and police cruisers and parked alongside several ambulances. The explosion had been large enough to blow out a wall, and the fire consumed the rest. The ballroom was on the west wing of the castle, away from the sleeping quarters. By some miracle, they'd managed to stop it before the flames destroyed everything. A few firefighters were hosing down a fresh layer of ash, while medics dragged bodies out of the destroyed castle.

When I pulled up to the ballroom and got out of my car, men were frantically digging through the rubble. An officer with soot on his cheek glared at me as I looked around. I decided to ask him some questions so I knew exactly what I was up against. "How many people were injured? Is His Highness okay? Is it true? Did the queen die?" I already knew Augustus was relatively fine. A few cuts and scrapes. A broken, bleeding heart. I still needed to play my part. Confused. Unaware. Disoriented.

I was rewarded with multiple gasps and wide eyes, but the simplest answer was from a middle-aged man wearing a leather jacket. "The situation is under control." The royal publicist probably gave everyone that scripted response.

I pulled my hand away from my face and quickly wiped my fake *tears*. It was not difficult to feign grief. I was a little shocked at the loss of life. Even if I'd seen my fair share of death, it didn't mean I wasn't affected by it. Though as my kill count climbed, the loss started to hollow.

Searching the space for Augustus, I expected him to be lying in the dirt, inconsolable and useless. But to my surprise, he was knee-deep in ash, plowing through piles of debris, with tears streaming down his face.

It was a strange sight to see. Adonis was at his back, helping him sort through the destruction. Maids with bloodshot eyes watched him with pity. Firefighters worked harder than ever, knowing that their king was barking orders and losing his mind.

"We have to fucking find her! Where the hell is Atticus?" he sobbed.

I observed him for a moment, *almost almost almost* feeling guilty for what I had to do.

But not quite. I'd never apologize for protecting Christine.

And that was exactly what I was doing.

"I'm right here, Augustus," I said.

Leo stood by a beam of wood, sawing it in half and

heaving. When I announced myself, he looked at me with pure, unadulterated *anger*. I didn't have time to deconstruct that look, but I had a feeling he'd talk to me later. I didn't have time for his temper tantrum now, though.

Augustus spun around, his eyes wide with fear. He pulled himself out of the wreckage and ran toward me, forgetting to wipe the ash off his face. "Where were you? Why haven't you been helping us?!" His hands grabbed onto me like he was drowning and I was his lifeline.

I opened and closed my mouth, surprised by his show of emotion. I watched as he wiped his nose with the back of his soot-covered hand. He was dripping with sweat and still wore the tuxedo he had on last night, though it was covered in cinders, now. When I didn't immediately answer, he sucked in a raspy breath, then looked over his shoulder to shout at onlookers. "Nobody stops digging. We *will* find her!"

"What are you doing?" I asked him. "You're going to hurt yourself."

He ran his shaky hands through his hair. "What am I doing? What are *you* doing? Christine is missing. That damn fire chief says I need to prepare for her to be dead. Dead, Atticus!"

I flinched. The idea of Christine being dead was

horrifying. Even though I knew she was safe, tucked in my bed and sleeping off the pain meds my personal doctor had given her, it still shook me to my core to imagine the alternative. The truth was, Lord Nathan could have easily killed her last night. We almost didn't escape. Which was exactly why she couldn't stay in the castle. No one could be trusted. "Augustus, you need to sit down," I said.

"How can you be so calm?!" he roared. "My mother is dead. Half the castle went up in flames last night. And no one knows where Christine is. What happened? You were dancing with her."

I pulled away from him and started pacing the ground, trying to look distraught. "The explosion separated us. People were running everywhere. I tried to find her, but the crowd pushed me out. I passed out from smoke inhalation and woke up in the hospital this morning. Are you sure she didn't get out?"

With each word, his voice rose. Louder and louder, he spoke. "She's not at the hospital, Atticus. The castle has been swept by Leo. And the security footage is being combed through now. No one saw her leave. She's gone. She's fucking gone!" He glanced at the police officers and the other firefighters who were trying to make sense of the situation. I made a mental note to have one of my hackers make sure there's no video of me putting

Christine in my car. Augustus pulled me toward him and dropped his voice. "Maybe they took her. Maybe everyone is in on this. We can't trust *anyone*."

He had no clue how close to the truth he was.

"It was chaotic last night, Augustus. It would have been impossible—"

He frowned, realizing the oddity of his outburst. "I…I'm trying to figure everything out." He looked at me with his brown eyes, ones that were filled with so much pain that I felt a little guilty for hurting him like this. "She hasn't answered any of my calls. The hospital is triple-checking their patients. If she were hurt, I would have been notified immediately."

I gave him a sad look, letting my mask of pain slowly dance across my expression. I'd never considered myself an actor, but being the head of a criminal organization made me good at lying.

"She's not at the hospital, Augustus," I said. "And you know it."

He looked at me with narrowed eyes, trying to make sense of what I was saying. "Then where is she?"

My eyes flickered to the destruction before us. "I-I think she's in there." I let my voice break for effect.

"No. No, she can't be. Not Christine, Atticus."

I had to drive the point home. "If she didn't get out…if she didn't get out, Augustus…"

His face darkened. "No." He shook his head, refusing to believe it.

It wasn't hard to pretend to be upset. I crouched in the dirt, holding my head in my hands as I listened to his words. She could've died last night. If I hadn't dragged her out of there, she would've burned alive in this damn castle that she hated so much. "She's gone," I said. My eyes watered as I imagined her lifeless body. Skin cold. Void eyes and limbs bent at odd angles.

Tears welled up in my eyes at the image. It was an outcome I refused to let happen.

I stood up and Augustus charged toward me, his lips twisted in a snarl. "Why didn't you save her!?" He shoved my chest, nearly knocking me over. "Why didn't you make sure she was safe? For all your talk of wanting to be there for her—of loving her—you failed!"

I didn't fail. Augustus was not willing to do what I did. I got her out of this castle for her own well-being. He would've kept her at his side and put her right in harm's way. But I couldn't trust him to take care of the woman I loved. At least, not yet. He had too many enemies breathing down his neck for reasons he wasn't even aware of yet. The secrets about his lineage died with his mother but still lived within me. I didn't know what Lord Nathan knew, and if word got out, Augustus would have too many enemies to count. I needed time to assess what rumors were flying around and get rid of Lord Nathan.

Augustus grabbed me and, to my shock, collapsed in my arms. "I failed her. I didn't *protect* her, Atticus." I was struck with indecision for a moment, not sure how to handle this, but I surprised myself by patting him on the back before squeezing him for a hug. "She can't be gone," he whispered.

I looked over him at the collection of people standing about, watching their king fall to his knees with grief. If we wanted to get back at Lord Nathan, Augustus would need to find his anger and make him pay. That was the only way. We couldn't let whispers about his weakness bleed through the kingdom.

"What are you all looking at!" I screamed. "Why aren't you digging?!"

A few men jumped into action and started moving a fallen beam. Leo wiped his eyes and glared at me. I needed to speak with him soon.

"Let's keep searching," I said. "We don't stop until the job is done. We'll find her."

Augustus pulled himself up and stumbled over to the rubble. "We'll find her," he whispered. "We have to. She can't be gone. She's strong, Atticus. If she's in there, we have to save her." He ran toward the rubble, ignoring the shouts from his guards yelling at him to stop. He grabbed onto a fallen pillar, pulling it off the ground. It was too heavy for him and he fell to his knees, dropping it. I stood and walked toward him, hovering in solidarity like a good friend *should*. "This isn't over," he exclaimed, screaming into the air. "We have to find her!"

I did this. I caused this mess, but I wasn't about to let her become a casualty to it. This was the only way.

"We'll keep looking," I said. "We'll keep digging." I kept my voice strong, even though I felt a surprising wave of guilt. I shook it off and looked back at the men working in the rubble. "Hurry up!" I yelled. "Find her!"

Augustus clawed at the dirt while tears streamed down his cheeks. "We'll find her," he murmured until his fingers bled. I watched him for a moment, observing with a sinking heart as he found the strength to stand. I was afraid that the weight of his grief would be too much for him to bear. But she was mine to protect. Not just from our enemies, but from the pain that lay within us. The shadows we couldn't escape. "Find her," he whispered, wiping at his tears. "I am going to find her," he said, as if convincing himself. "She can't be dead. She's too damn stubborn to die."

I nodded without response. I let him believe what he wanted. I watched him as he returned to the wreckage.

He continued to dig, heaving blocks of stone off the building.

"Augustus," I called. He ignored me, continuing with his work. "Augustus," I said hesitantly. I looked at the debris and then back at him. He stopped for a moment and looked at what remained of the castle. Dusty rubble covered the whole area, soot and ash lingering in the air. The castle that his great-grandfather built was partially destroyed and possibly left a grave-yard buried beneath the debris.

"What?" he snapped.

I let out a shaky breath. "I want to find the person responsible for this." *And you should want to find him, too. Get mad, Augustus. Get furious.*

He looked at me with teary eyes.

"I want to find her *first*."

And with those words, I positioned myself at his side, digging through the dirt, imagining what would have happened to my Little Monster had I not gotten her out in time.

Chapter Two

With a hiss of pain in my chest, I slammed my palm against the bedroom door. I had burns on the back of my arm, and my hair smelled like smoke. "Let me out of here!" I shouted, though my tone was hoarse. Every word was like knives against my sore throat.

"Mr. DuPont will be back shortly," the guard on the other side said, though his voice was muffled.

I let out a huff, then choked on a few sputtering coughs. My lungs felt hot and tight. I couldn't taste anything. My nose was too full of the acrid smoke and the smell of my own burning flesh.

"Why am I here? Where is everyone?!" I asked, but

the man didn't answer me. Whoever stood watch was under strict instructions to keep quiet.

I took in the large space. There was a king-size bed with a rumpled comforter in a deep shade of burgundy. The closet was full of fashionable, expensive suits, and there was a photo of Atticus and me on the nightstand. It was the blurry photo of us embracing in a twisted kiss. The same photo he'd shown August. My eyes focused on it the moment I woke up and shot out of bed.

What happened after I left the castle last night? Who attacked us?

I stormed over to the tall windows and glared at the city outside. In the far distance, I could see a cloud of smoke lingering where the castle was. My lungs clenched at the sight. Flashes of fire and Isabelle's body in my mind's eye made me tremble.

Isabelle was *dead*.

Soft tears fell down my cheeks. She'd been a maternal figure to me and the last connection I had to my own mother. She wasn't always kind, but she'd saved me during one of my weakest moments. It was strange to resent her and mourn her all at once. She'd brought me back here. She'd sent me away.

And now she was gone.

My lips were chapped, and I was breathing heavily. My tongue felt like it was three times its normal size.

I looked out the window once more. Atticus lived on the top floor of a tall tower overlooking all the people of Aldrich. He was a king in his own right with this view. I wore one of his button-up shirts, and I traced the hem with my index finger, wondering who changed my clothes, who bandaged my arm, and why I was locked inside.

I needed a phone. August and Leo were probably worried sick about me.

Or maybe they were in on this too? Maybe it wasn't safe?

Maybe something had happened to them.

There wasn't a damn television in the bedroom, and I had no phone, no belongings whatsoever. I hated not knowing what was going on, and the pounding in my head got worse with each second.

I felt trapped.

I *hated* feeling trapped.

As I knelt low on the ground, I listened for sounds outside, steadying my breathing. Crawling over to the nightstand, I suddenly realized I needed a weapon.

Hudson's words flickered through my mind. *You should always have a weapon, Christine. If you can't find one, make one.*

I grabbed the framed photo and broke the glass on the ground, the shards scattering and digging into the carpet. The photo of Atticus and me looked even more unperfect. Blurred. Cracked.

Wrong.

I grabbed the biggest piece of glass and clenched it in my fist, letting the sharp edge dig into my palm. Crimson blood dripped down my wrist as I pressed my back against the wall and waited.

And waited.

The sun started to set, and my stomach growled. Moody twilight cast warm light in his room, the edge of darkness seeping in my soul.

Isabelle was dead.

I didn't know where August or Leo were. If they were alive. If they were injured.

My hold on the glass tightened, sending a fresh wave of blood onto the floor, staining Atticus's shirt. Staining my heart.

My vision was blurry from tears, and my eyes watered faster than I could blink them away. My heartbeat was pounding in my ears, my breath rattled in my lungs. "I have to get out of here," I said to no one. My voice sounded like I'd swallowed a handful of rocks. Fat tears fell slow and heavy, taking with them chunks of my will and desire to live.

When the doorknob twisted, my eyes glazed over into that numb familiarity that saved my life three years ago. "Christine?"

Atticus stormed inside and circled the bed. When he found me sitting on the floor and covered in blood, a fiery determination took over his expression. He was covered head to toe in ash, his pristine suit damn near ruined from the cinders. His curly hair was an ashy gray from all the debris, and the smudges of dirt blended in with the tattoos creeping up his neck. "What happened?"

His strong hand wrapped around my wrist, forcing me to release the glass. It landed on the carpet, and my eyes sliced up to his. "I felt trapped," I whispered. "Where were you? What happened? Are August and Leo okay? Is Isabelle…" The more I spoke, the more my throat hurt. Another painful cough erupted and Atticus placed his hand on my back as I hacked.

"I'm sorry," he whispered, his voice low and concerned. "Christine, I'm so sorry." He lowered himself onto the floor, pulling me into his arms. It was a natural reaction, needing a familiar place to brace myself. His arms circled me, his hand stroking my back in slow, steady circles. The warmth of his body soaked into my skin, and I leaned against his chest, taking in his scent. He smelled like ash and burnt wood, smoke and death. His hand on my back felt so good, soothing me. Protecting me. "Isabelle died in the fire. It was fast. She didn't suffer." His voice was like a gentle caress. "August and Leo are fine," he said, his tone keeping my heart from exploding in my chest. "I'm sorry," he whispered.

"Isabelle," I said, closing my eyes. I could picture her face so well, as if she were sitting in front of me. She was always so calm, so gentle. "Isabelle is dead," I repeated, as if saying it out loud would make it real.

"You sound terrible. I'll have my personal doctor come back and listen to your lungs. I'm worried…"

I tried to swallow, but my mouth was too dry. "Is that who did this?" I asked while holding up my bandaged arm.

He stared at my arm as if my injuries personally offended him. "Yes. Have you eaten the food I left for you? Drank any water?"

"I didn't really have the stomach for eating. I woke up in a strange place without my clothes and bandaged up."

His gaze softened. "I'm sorry, Christine. I wanted to be here."

But he wasn't here. I scowled. "Tell me what happened. Tell me *everything*. Where are the others? Why aren't they here?"

Atticus got up and went over to a cart by the door.

He grabbed a glass of water and a towel, then came back over to me. "Take a drink and I'll tell you. Then let me wash your hand."

I took a drink, but my throat burned, and I coughed again. "I feel like I'm dying," I managed to say, but at least there was no blood in my mouth. Atticus exhaled and his lips pressed into a thin line. "No, you're not dying. Not if I have anything to say about it."

I swallowed a few more times and then let the water soothe my throat. "Okay. Tell me. Tell me everything."

"Your engagement party was attacked. Three bombs went off," he explained, pulling me up from the floor. "Do you remember anything?"

Nausea swirled in my gut with each image that popped into my head. The smell of smoke, the taste of ashes, the sound of yelling…it overwhelmed my senses. "I remember some of it…Atticus…where were you today? Why did I wake up alone?"

"Drink more water and I'll tell you."

I rolled my eyes and took a sip. The cool liquid felt good against my throat, and before I knew it, I was gulping it down.

"Good girl," Atticus said. His praise sent a shiver down my spine. He waited until I was sucking down another mouthful when he spoke. "I was with Augustus, digging through the rubble, searching for your body."

His words shocked me, and I choked on the liquid I was drinking, then started coughing again. "What?!" I rasped out through painful wheezes.

He waited for me to stop sputtering before responding. "I got you out of there last night, Christine. You passed out in my car. I summoned a doctor, and he gave you pain medication. I almost *lost* you. Someone attacked your engagement party. I couldn't risk—"

"Does August think I'm *dead*?" I asked incredulously. "What about Leo?"

"Yes. Both of them," he answered.

"Why would you do that, Atticus?" I hissed. "Why the hell would you put them through that?"

"It was the only way I could keep you safe, Little Monster. I didn't have a choice, and I refuse to apologize for it. I'm sorry you woke up here alone, but I'm not sorry for keeping you alive."

His reasoning was so logical and methodical it made me sick. My eyes narrowed and my throat burned again, but this time, because I thought I was going to throw up. "Nothing is safe. Not anymore. You lied to them. You made them think I was dead!" I couldn't hold it back anymore as tears spilled down my cheeks and I started sobbing. Irrational anger bubbled up, pushing past the fear.

He grabbed my hand and the glass of water. While

pouring it onto my palm and dabbing it with a towel, he spoke. "They have to believe you're dead if I'm going to keep you from getting hurt again."

I noticed the way he wouldn't meet my gaze. "Who wants to hurt me, Atticus?"

"Whoever attacked the castle last night. I'm guessing Lord Nathan."

His words made my soul seize. "Atticus, August *needs* me. His mother died in that explosion. I saw her…" My voice trailed off as I thought back to the sight of her battered body soaked with blood, flames caressing her skin. She'd always looked so put together. So *perfect and polished*.

"You're going to stay here, Christine."

I shook my head. "No. You can't do this to me. I want to leave."

Atticus dropped the towel and we both stood up. My legs were shaking from adrenaline. This wasn't right. "You're staying here," he said. "That's final."

"No," I replied while pushing his chest with my good hand. "Atticus, I'm not——"

"You will, Christine!" His scream made me jump and take a step back. "You will stay here where it's safe, because I can't stand the thought of losing you." He took a step toward me, then pressed me against the wall. "Because I just saw what happens when you *die.* I just saw how destroyed Augustus and Leo are. I just saw how it feels to lose you, Little Monster. And I'll let it be their reality, but I refuse for it to be mine."

I gasped and swallowed hard. Atticus had never revealed so much emotion to me before. My skin prickled with goose bumps, and I gripped his arms. "Atticus." His eyes glistened, and I could tell he was trying so hard to stay in control. "You can't do this. It's not right. It's…insane."

"I can and I will," he said through gritted teeth. "I've been pushed to my limit, and I refuse to lose you." His grip on my arms tightened.

Caught between rage and fear, I managed to whisper. "Please don't do this. Please."

He slammed his lips to mine, his tongue like ash, his mouth like fire. He pressed his soot-covered frame against mine, and I inhaled the smell of smoke on his skin, melted against his hot body.

"I'm not staying here," I said between raspy kisses.

"You will," he replied while propping his thigh between my legs.

I tugged on his hair, exposing his neck as I buried my lips against his warm, dirty skin. "I'll fight you."

He tugged at the buttons of my shirt, sending them scattering across the floor as he ripped the soft material from my body. "I'll take every fucking hit, Little Monster."

My nipples pebbled, and he pinched them, rolling the sensitive tips between his rough thumbs and index fingers. "I'll escape, Atticus."

"You won't."

I ground against his thigh, moaning as he sunk lower to kiss my exposed skin. My breasts, my stomach. My inner thigh. He was on his knees before me, his heavy gaze looking up at me as if I was precious. "I will, Atticus. Don't make me hurt you."

He stared at my center and pried my legs apart with his strong hands. "I like to hurt," he replied before burying his face against my pussy. I gasped, sucking in air as his hot breath washed over me in waves. His hand lifted my thigh over his shoulder, and I curled around him, feeling needy and angry all at once.

But I wanted to feel *alive*. I wanted to prove I was really here and I wasn't going to play dead for him. My hands threaded through his brown hair, and I tugged on the strands as he flicked my clit with his tongue.

He dug his fingers into my muscles and held me still, tasting me. *Devouring me.* It was precious and damning all at once. I hated the way he commanded my body, because just like everything else in my life, he was in complete control. He had me whimpering and writing against him, soaking up the feel of his mouth against me, savoring the way he murmured filthy words.

"You taste so sweet for someone so angry, Little Monster."

"Fuck you," I groaned. I didn't hate Atticus. I hated feeling like my life wasn't my own. My body wasn't my own.

The damn air in my lungs was a lie, and he was stealing every breath.

"I'll fuck you," he said before moving his hand and shoving his thick finger inside of me, thrusting so beautifully my soul quivered.

"Shut up."

He laughed, the hearty sound like staccato waves against my clit.

My exhausted limbs felt too damn tense. His heat, too potent. The world was a chaotic mess, and I couldn't see the light. I couldn't…I couldn't…I needed this. I needed him. I needed him to give me the illusion of control. I needed to be able to say it, even if I couldn't believe it. "I hate you."

"You do. But you love me, too." He pulled his fingers from my body, and his teeth nipped at my clit before his fingers sunk once more inside of me with such force I felt my pulse in my ears. The pressure was intense and I cried out, tingles forming on the back of my neck as my body came alive. Every cell in my body sparked to life.

He devoured me in a vengeful way, his lips and tongue making love to me in a way I'd never known I needed. He held me still, and I curled around him, the pressure building inside of me. The pressure to feel something. Anything real.

He stopped for a brief moment and looked up at me. "Why are you still crying?" he asked.

"Because."

"Because of what?"

"Because you're so fucking good at this, and I don't want you to be."

His laughter was primal, and I felt it against my skin. He pulled away, his eyes bright as his fingers traced my bottom lip. "I know you love me," he said.

"You don't know shit, Atticus."

"I know you."

He went back to licking my clit.

I felt my orgasm building as he pushed his fingers in and out of me. Harder and harder. His other hand gripped my thigh, and I writhed, taking everything he was giving. Stealing what was his.

I was drowning in his voice. His body. His scent. His everything. Even when I closed my eyes, I could see him. I could fucking see him. And it pissed me off.

The pressure became overwhelming, and I could feel my eyes roll back in my head. "Fuck you," I cursed. And damn, he felt good. So good it made doing this even harder.

I lowered my leg and shoved him back as hard as I could, just before he could rip an orgasm out of me. He landed on the ground in the shards of glass but didn't make a sound. My arousal glistened on his lips, and his eyes were like haunting black orbs of power.

"I'm not letting you get away with this," I growled before straddling his body. I bent at the hips, pressing my hand to his throat. With him at my mercy, I felt powerful. "You don't get to taste me, Atticus. You don't get to *control* me. I'm tired of everyone staking a claim. I belong to myself. I'm *alive*."

A smile crossed his mouth, surprising me. "Yes, Little Monster."

"Don't look so pleased," I said. "You've started a war in your home. I won't submit easily. You made me a monster, and now I'll show you just how capable I am. I'll show *everyone*."

He arched his eyebrow, his smug smile fading. "I know how capable you are," he said. "You think I don't see how powerful—how *perfect*—you are? I know you can fight your own battles, but it doesn't mean I won't protect you." The intensity in his gaze bounced between pain and pleasure.

"If you thought I was powerful, you wouldn't hide me away and let the rest of the world think I was dead. You wouldn't lie to the men I love, Atticus."

"You love me, too."

"I'm not sure I can love someone who treats me like this," I admitted, and the mask he wore finally cracked. I saw a flicker of fear flash across his eyes.

"You can. And you will."

"I hope you enjoyed the taste of me, because I'm never letting you touch me again," I spat.

He licked his lips, savoring my arousal for a moment before speaking. "Go ahead. Fight it. It'll make claiming you so much sweeter."

I got off of him and scowled. "I'm not staying here."

"Go shower, Christine. Then you need to eat. Tomorrow, we're having dinner with my parents."

"What? Your parents?"

"Yes," he said while sitting up and picking a shard of glass off his suit. "We have some things we need to discuss with them. I can assure you, they're just as good at keeping secrets as I am, and they agree that keeping you here where it's safe is best for everyone."

My scowl was so heavy I felt like I could collapse.

"Of course they do." My anger was like venom, infecting everyone.

I picked up the photo of us kissing and stared at it for a moment, the weight of his gaze pressing down on me. "This is a lie, you know," I said softly.

"What? The picture or us?"

I ripped it up and let the tattered pieces fall to the floor. "Both."

And with those parting words, I stormed off to the bathroom and slammed the door shut, his laughter a haunting reminder that I was locked here while two men who I loved thought I was gone forever.

Chapter Three

ATTICUS

I didn't want to be at the fucking castle. I didn't want to drag a king out of the pits of grief and make sure he didn't drink himself to death. And I definitely preferred my warm bed, where an angry Little Monster was curled up with the blankets wrapped tightly around her, a wall of pillows separating us.

As if feather pillows would hold me back.

The only thing that kept me from prying apart her thighs and sinking into Christine's hot warmth was that I never wanted her to associate me with the demons that stole her precious innocence. Even though I knew she wanted me just as badly as I wanted her, when we finally collided, she would look me in the eye and *beg*.

So I was here. At the damn castle. Inhaling the remnants of smoke in the air and trying not to punch something. At least my anger would help convince Augustus that I was grieving. He liked to wallow. I liked to kill people.

I parked my car and walked up the steps, where a line of armed guards glared at me. Leo appeared at the top of the stairs, his arms crossed over his chest and that damn long hair of his flowing in the wind. "We need to talk," he huffed.

I observed him openly. He had dark circles under his eyes and a snarl on his lips. He looked tired as hell, but not like a tortured, grieving man who lost a woman he cared about.

"Let's talk," I replied.

He stormed through the doors, then immediately turned down a hallway. I followed after him, prepared for whatever misguided bullshit he wanted to spew. I'd known plenty of men like Leo Winthrop. He was a hero. A protective asshole. He liked saving the damsels in distress. We were complete opposites. Yes, I'd save the pretty girl from her own demise, but I'd also fuck her raw without guilt. Claim her like the dragon she was running from.

I followed him into an empty security room where monitors lined the wall. He nodded at the screen, then spoke. "I already cleared the footage of you putting Christine in your town car the night of the explosion."

So he knew? Not surprising.

I pondered how I wanted to play this for a moment before speaking. "I suppose I should thank you." *Should* being the operative word. But he had ulterior motives for bringing me here today, and I'd play along until I figured out his game.

"You should *definitely* be thanking me." Leo crossed his arms and leaned against the wall.

"And yet, I won't." I crossed my arms, mimicking his stance. "You're a smart man. You know this was the best course of action. You did it for her, not for me."

"I had to." Leo's eyes glowed with determination, and he took a step toward me. "She wasn't safe here."

Easy enough. I had work to do and he wasn't worth my time. "So we're on the same page. Good talk."

"Is she okay?" The concern in his voice was suffocating.

"Burns on her arm and a sore throat. Doctor said she'll be fine, though." I eyed him as he sighed in relief. I couldn't blame him. I'd had the same reaction. When I first pulled her from the building, I'd thought the worst. "Just to be clear. You're not calling me here to try to convince me to tell Augustus, right?" The guard didn't like his king, but he had a code of ethics and nasty little morals that were truly an inconvenience to men like me.

"Of course not," he replied with a scowl. "Christine needs to be as far away from him and this castle as possible."

"Then I don't understand why you summoned me here. I'm a busy man. I've got to go make sure your king isn't trying to overdose from the guilt."

I turned to leave, but he reached out and grabbed my shoulder. "Not so fast."

I aggressively shrugged him off and turned back to look at him. "What?"

"I want to see her."

An easy enough request, but I wouldn't allow it. "No."

"Why not?" He looked like someone had just stolen his favorite toy.

"Because I don't trust you. Christine may like you, but I sure as hell don't. You're going to be a good little shadow and stay here with Augustus. Keep him safe so she doesn't rip both our balls off. You know she'd be devastated if anything happened to the fucker. And if you're lucky, I'll give you the occasional update about how good her lips feel wrapped around my cock." I gave him a smug grin, the only kind of grin we DuPont men knew. The kind that said I'd fuck him up if not for the fact that Christine enjoyed his company. "I think that covers it." I turned to leave, but Leo was a persistent little bastard.

He grabbed my shoulder once more. "I want to see her," he growled. "I *deserve* to see her." I tensed, ready to punch him right in his green eyes. They'd look better bloody. "I need to know that she's okay," he added in a quieter voice.

I loomed over him and glared. "She's doing great. Happy. Healthy. Thrilled to be with me."

His gaze roamed my expression. "You're lying. I bet she's pissed as hell at you. I bet she *hates* you."

I grabbed his shoulders and pinned him to the wall. "I'm going to let that go because you helped me erase the footage, but if you say that one more time, I'll rip your throat out with my bare hands. Understand?" I punctuated my sentence by releasing him and tossing him aside.

He rubbed his shoulder where I'd gripped him. "Did I strike a nerve?" he taunted. "She's pissed at you. Admit it. If you let me see her, maybe—"

"You think *you* could get her to talk? You're barely man enough to act on your feelings for her. I bet when she looks at you, all she feels is pity."

He balled his fists at his side and took a step closer to me. "You're going to take me to her."

I cocked my brow. I didn't think the poor man had it in him. "Or what?"

"Or I'll tell Augustus that she's alive. And you can try to kill me, but if I go missing, I have a contact that will inform the king of what you're up to—"

I knew Leo wasn't close to too many people. It was easy to deduce who he might have told. "Your mother? Or your sweet little sister? I could kill both of them." I shrugged. It didn't bother me to tie up loose ends.

If he was worried about my threat, he didn't show it. Once again, the golden retriever of a man surprised me. "Your threats might mean a lot in your world, but they're empty promises in mine. I don't care how much power you have or how deadly you think you are. You're going to let me see Christine."

He poked me in the chest with his index finger, and I debated snapping it off and shoving it up his ass. I considered my options for a moment. Something about his nonreaction to my threat told me that Leo didn't tell his mother or sister about this, which meant someone in the castle knew. "I thought you wanted to keep her safe?" I questioned.

"I do," he snapped. "Which is why I'm demanding to see her. I want to make sure she's taken care of. I don't trust you, Atticus. At least with Augustus, I know I'll be here to protect her. I'd prefer for her to stay with you, but I want to keep an eye on her, too." He pinned me with a hard stare.

I didn't know why, but I believed him. I had no way of knowing if he was bluffing or not, but I assumed he wasn't. If I didn't let him see Christine, he would tell the king. And then I'd have two problems to deal with. Not a situation I wanted to be in. "You won't try anything stupid?"

"I want to see her, Atticus. The only thing I'm going to do is ensure she's okay."

I crossed my arms and looked at him, trying to figure out if he was trying to make me feel guilty for keeping him from seeing her or if he really was worried about her. I wanted to trust him, but I didn't know him well enough to be certain.

Insufferable bastard. He'd put me in a hard position, and I was feeling positively possessive, but if he was so damn determined, I'd let him. Christine might like Leo Winthrop, but he still needed to prove his worthiness to me. "Fine. But give me a few days to get her settled."

"I'm coming by tonight."

My jaw clenched. I glared at Leo and considered how I might kill him. Piece by piece. "You'll come *when I summon you*, or I'll deliver your body to her in a box."

He smiled at me. "And then she'd never speak to you again."

Fucking asshole.

"Give me a few days," I said again. "That's my final offer." *I needed more time to get her to forgive me.* I had plans to make her feel more in control at our dinner with my parents.

"Fine," he gritted. I smirked. He knew when he was up against an immovable force. Truthfully, it was probably good for me to have an ally on the inside who knew about Christine. I didn't want to burn any bridges, even if I wasn't sure where Leo stood in this fucked up dynamic.

"Thank you," he breathed, and I knew his relief was genuine. At least he cared about Christine. At least she had people to keep her safe. Maybe it would take all of us to protect her.

To my utter surprise, I found Augustus sitting at his desk, shuffling through papers and barking orders at Adonis. He was wearing all black, the typical clothes for mourning, but his hair was a mess and there was a plate of uneaten food on a tray. "You're here," he said, glancing up at me before pouring over his work once more. His eyes were bloodshot, and he was so pale that he looked sickly.

"Surprised to find you in your office," I noted before sitting down.

"Did you do what I asked?" His tone was bland, devoid of any emotion. Robotic, almost.

Letting out a long sigh, I answered. "Lord Nathan wasn't at his home in St. Idyll. No one has seen him since the attack."

Augustus clenched his fist until his knuckles turned white. "I want him *here* so I can question him properly. So I can *kill* the motherfucker."

My eyes widened in surprise. I'd expected Augustus to be a blubbering, grieving idiot, drinking away his sorrows and frozen from inaction. "We want the same thing. I have all the men I can spare looking for him."

"Good. I can't wait to rip the skin from his bones."

Surprisingly, I respected Augustus more than ever at that moment. He was broken. He was angry. But he was still trying to be the king. "I'll bring him to you. No use risking your life tracking him down."

"As if my life means anything." He reached into a pocket and pulled out a polished silver pocket watch, which he checked absently. "I have a meeting with the lords in an hour. They're going to have to wait a little bit." He set it down, then rubbed his temples. "They want to talk about plans. How I'm going to navigate the attack. Where I want to send our armies. Th-the funerals." The grief was evident in Augustus's voice. He shook his head, like he couldn't believe what he was saying. "I don't want to talk about those things. I just want to kill Nathan. I want him to suffer." He seemed to lose himself in his thoughts, staring blankly at nothing. He looked up at me, and the sad, defeated look on his face made me feel like an even bigger piece of shit.

"You don't have to have this meeting if you're not ready." I didn't want to see him debilitated. He wasn't the incompetent prince I'd thought he was. He was trying to hold on to his kingdom and his sanity.

"You're wrong," he countered. "I have to go to the meeting. To prove that I'm doing my part. I cannot show weakness." His eyes shot to mine, and I saw a hardened glint there. His red eyes lifted to meet mine. "You'll let me be the one to kill him, Atticus. I know you want revenge as much as I do, but as your king, I demand you let me do the honor of sending him to hell."

Interesting. "You never really had a taste for killing," I noted.

"I never felt angry enough to want to actually kill someone." He tapped his chest, just over where his heart would be if he had one. "I still feel her. I spent three years without her, Atticus, and now every second feels like eternity."

Few people had ever said such things to me. I'd built a persona of strength and stoic reserve. We didn't discuss our feelings or pain. We fought with bloody knuckles and buried our enemies. I might have even pretended that I didn't understand his anguish. But I did. I was living in that hell with him. "I know," I said.

Augustus scoffed, glaring at me. "I know you do. That's why you're going to let me be the one to end his life."

He had every right to kill Nathan. He was the king. He was the one who had to rule over all of this. I just wanted to go back to my tower. Wait for Christine to forgive me. Forget everything else.

But I couldn't let him become a killer. Taking a life was a slippery slope, one Christine was navigating. I was protecting him and he didn't even know it.

He got up to pour himself a glass of water, and I watched him drink it. I didn't even think the privileged king drank anything but champagne. "I can't make that kind of promise, Augustus. You're not the only person enraged by what he's done."

And I wouldn't let my *friend* slip into that dangerous pit. Once you took your first life, you were never the same.

"You will. You'll give me this one thing, Atticus, so help me God—"

"Don't threaten me with a higher power neither one of us believes in. Where was God when she burned in that ballroom, Augustus?" I turned my head and stared at the wall. I was the one who got her to safety. *I* was the one keeping her safe. And I'd continue to do so.

Augustus shook his head, angrily glaring at me. "I want to hurt him."

I tipped my chin up. "So do I." Lord Nathan would regret ever threatening the people I cared about.

"I want to kill him." Augustus's voice was quiet, calm, but layered with the promise of revenge. "It might be the only way I can ever feel close to her again." I knew how he felt, but I couldn't let him do it. Not now. Not when his grief was still so fresh. "I want to hurt him," he repeated. "And if you do not let me, I will kill every last person in this kingdom." He leaned forward, his voice dropping to a dangerous whisper. "I will kill them all, Atticus. I swear it." His promise was a bounty, a brutal promise of what would happen if I did not comply. "Give me this," he pleaded. "Let me do this." Augustus was no longer the comical, pompous prince, but a brutal, bloodthirsty, vengeful man. I briefly wondered if I'd created a monster. If we shared more in common than I realized.

I changed the subject. "Have you found out why Lord Nathan has made it his mission to bring you down? He's spreading rumors that you aren't a worthy heir. Leaking gossip." I was fishing for information.

He scoffed and moved back to his seat. "It doesn't matter what rumors he spreads. It doesn't matter if I'm qualified or not. I'm the next in line. King Frederick's blood runs through my veins, no matter how much I hate him. Rumors don't mean anything."

Except that was a lie. It wasn't King Frederick's blood running through his veins. He was born of something far more sinister. Far more…deadly. He was an heir in his own right, but not to this castle and certainly not to the Crown.

I leaned forward. "Tell me, Augustus, why are you here? Working? Are you trying to be *qualified* for the job?"

He sat down, his shoulders dipping as he stared at the stacks of papers on his table. "Crying won't bring her back. Getting fucked up won't, either. The only thing that feels right is killing the man responsible, and I won't rest until I do."

That was exactly what I wanted to hear. Augustus had to get mad and man the fuck up so Christine could be safe. I was capable of many things, but it would take all of us to bury the secrets Queen Isabelle and I harbored. "I can relate to the sentiment," I replied.

He eyed me with heavy scrutiny, dragging his gaze over my suit and the careful expression I wore. "You seem to be handling it well. I figured you'd have burned down half the kingdom by now."

He was right. I needed to be angrier. If Christine were *actually* dead, I'd be a lethal force to be reckoned with. Sitting here in his office wasn't how I would respond to losing the love of my life. I'd be out there, bringing the world to its knees. "I'm actually on my way to do just that. Lord Nathan had plenty of friends in court. I'll be meeting with them and seeing what information I can get. I just stopped by to…" My voice trailed off. Admitting that I was worried about him made a sour taste fill my mouth.

Augustus let out a dark, humorless chuckle. "Babysit me? Make sure I wasn't hurting myself from the grief? No, Atticus. I'm not crying in a corner or taking a handful of pills. I need you to do your fucking job."

I nodded. I needed to be cruel. Atticus DuPont didn't talk about his feelings or aimlessly flounder without a plan. I was the man who watched Christine for years. Coordinated her training. Made every aspect of her life simple. "Right. Christine was the one that took care of you." I watched the pain hit his expression.

He clutched his stomach, as if my words were a blow to the gut. "You're not my responsibility. You were hers. And now she's gone."

"Get out," he snapped.

"Why? So you can sit at your desk and pretend to do something? So you can feel better about losing the only girl probably capable of loving you? Make idle threats we both know you won't fulfill? Are you going to let me do *all* your dirty work? Just sit here feeling productive until it's time to put a bullet in Lord Nathan's skull? Or are you going to get your knuckles bruised and burn your own fucking kingdom to the ground to avenge her?"

"I have a funeral to plan!" he shouted while standing up. He slammed a fist on the top of his desk. "*Two* fucking funerals."

"Then plan them, Augustus. Mourn what could have been while I kill the man that stole her from both of us."

I got up and walked out of the room, breathing a sigh of relief the moment I was away from him. It was in my nature to be aggressive and vicious.

It wasn't in my nature to feel bad about it.

So why did I?

Chapter Four

CHRISTINE

"**I**s that what you're wearing to dinner with my parents, Little Monster?" Atticus asked with a smirk while looking me up and down. I was wearing wrinkled silk pajamas with the buttons misaligned and shorts that were far too short for a formal dinner with the DuPonts. My blonde hair was a wavy, tangled mess.

"I'm not going," I replied, my nose tipped high up in the air.

Atticus walked over to me. I was staring out the window, looking off in the distance at the scorched castle. I could practically *feel* August pacing the floors, grieving me. I hated it.

"And to think I got you a present," he mused at my back, his hot breath washing over me.

Every muscle in my body tensed. With a heavy exhale, I forced myself to succumb to that numb plane of existence that didn't lust after Atticus. That didn't *love* him. And then I threw my elbow back, knowing it would connect with his throat and send him gasping for air.

But thick fingers wrapped around the joint, blocking me. His dark laughter rang in my ears, and the soft cushions of his lips whispered against my skin. "Good try, Little Monster."

"What's my present? A tombstone?" I gritted angrily, hating how the feel of him behind me made my legs weak.

"I told Leo if you're a good girl, I'll let him visit," he purred.

My eyes widened, and I spun around. "Leo?"

Atticus preened at my excitement, making me instantly wary. "He's smarter than I gave him credit for. Realized I was lying almost instantly."

I pursed my lips. "He'll tell August."

"No," Atticus said calmly. "He won't. Because he agrees with me. You're safer here, Christine. Until all of this is under control."

Of course Leo agreed with Atticus. He'd been

trying to get me out of that damn castle since the moment I arrived. "Then I don't want to see him."

Atticus clicked his tongue. "Don't be like that, sweetheart. He is dying to see you. I wasn't going to let him, but he seemed quite determined. Poor man has been worried sick."

I cleared my throat. "He has?"

Atticus nodded. "He has. Now, I don't mind if you attend dinner like this, but you might be more comfortable in something else. Would you like for me to pick out a dress for you? I remember how much you enjoyed the last time I did."

And just like that, I found myself hating Atticus again. "Nope," I replied, popping the *p*. "I'm comfortable in this."

"If you insist," he replied before grabbing my arm and pulling me toward him. I crashed against his chest and looked up at him. "You infuriate me," I growled.

"Does anger turn you on, Little Monster?" he asked before gripping my hips. I could feel his hard length pressing against my stomach. "Because I happen to love the way your mouth presses into a thin line. Makes me want to pry it open with my *cock*."

I licked my lips and stared at him for a moment, my breaths forcing my chest to rise and fall with heady desire. "Fuck you, Atticus."

He grinned devilishly. "My mother is going to love you."

"I'm not going, Atticus," I insisted.

"You will if you want to see Leo. And I know you want to see him. He owes you a kiss, does he not?"

"I won't be kissing anyone who treats me like an ignorant doll to be controlled," I gritted.

Atticus laughed once more. "You just let them kiss your pretty pussy, right?" He licked his lips to emphasize his point, making my stomach clench.

I shoved at him again, but his quick hands wrapped around my wrist. "If you want to see him, you'll come with me. My parents have always loved you."

I let out a sigh. I'd met his parents quite a few times when I was a teen. They were always kind to me, but I felt that something was always *off* about them. "Atticus, I don't like being bribed."

"But you do like being informed. You've been trapped in this room all day. Come with me. I promise it'll be worth your while. We can discuss the progress we've made in tracking down Lord Nathan and what his plans are. The sooner we take him out, the sooner you can join the world of the living. Plus, Leo has been with Augustus. You can ask him all about your precious king."

He did have a point. Hiding in my room wasn't

accomplishing anything, and if I left, maybe I could figure out an escape route. "Fine. But I'm not changing. You don't get to dress me up like a toy, Atticus."

"Of course, Little Monster. Whatever you desire."

I followed Atticus out of the room, and I openly took in the forest green paint on the walls and the masculine artwork. Atticus's living room was manly and moody, tasteful with brown leather sofas and a flatscreen mounted to the wall. Green plaid pillows that looked soft and cozy decorated a burgundy accent chair, and the vintage rug on the floor looked soft.

He had a large modern kitchen with towering cabinets and an industrial stove top. The extremely large island had ten barstools lined up. "This way," he said as I observed a guard standing in the corner.

Another hallway led to a large dining room with crown molding and detailed tiled ceilings. The ornate oak table sat at least sixteen people.

Elizabeth DuPont was sitting in a chair, scrolling on her cell phone with a smirk, and her husband, Theodore DuPont, was sipping whiskey at the head of the table. Both of their eyes snapped to me the moment we walked through the door. "Oh darling, your arm!" Elizabeth exclaimed while standing up. She wore a monochromatic beige pantsuit, and her hair was pulled back into a chic bun. The gold hoop earrings she wore bounced as she practically sprinted over to me in her designer heels. I stiffened when she wrapped her willowy arms around me and squeezed. "I was so worried about you and sweet Atty. I'm glad you got out of there safely. This whole mess is so disheartening." She pulled away and looked at me with sparkling brown eyes lined with long lashes.

"Let the poor girl breathe, Lizzy," Theodore said with a chuckle that reminded me of Atticus. As Elizabeth hugged me, I looked at Atticus's father with discerning eyes, noting the burgundy tie around his neck and the designer suit he wore. Theodore was tall like his son and had a commanding presence. His full head of hair was speckled with gray strands, and the gold cufflinks on his wrist sparkled under the chandeliers.

Elizabeth released me to hug her son. "Hello, darling. How was Augustus today? Poor thing."

It baffled me that all of them knew what their son was scheming and didn't seem bothered by it. But the DuPonts were adept at keeping secrets and treating people like moving chess pieces on a board they bought.

"He's determined to find Lord Nathan," Atticus replied while eyeing me.

We were all determined. I wanted nothing more

than to kill him the same way I murdered his brother. End the entire damn family line.

"We all are, son," Theodore said. "Have a seat. The food looks delicious." He held his hand out, presenting the table as if he'd spent all day in the kitchen making it. I knew the DuPonts had their own team of maids, cooks, drivers, and assistants. Not to mention the hundreds of armed guards in their arsenal.

Elizabeth DuPont looped her arm through mine and pulled me toward the chair right beside hers, sitting me down and pouring me a glass of water. "I just can't believe all of this. It's horrific."

"Darling, don't get worked up. You know how your nerves can get when you're too excited." Theodore's tone was cautionary.

Elizabeth huffed. "I just hate that Christine is going through this. I'm glad we have the resources to protect her during such a trying time. It's truly awful what Lord Nathan is doing." She turned to look at her son, who sat in the chair directly across from me. "You'll keep sweet Lady Abernathy safe, won't you?"

Atticus locked eyes with me. "Of course, Mother."

She beamed. "Just like your father. Always taking care of the women that hold your heart." She then winked at her husband, who offered her a bright smile.

This was so strange. They were acting like Atticus

and I were together, when I was engaged to the king. I felt the need to defend August even though he wasn't here. "My *fiancé* thinks the worst. I'm very upset with how things are being handled right now. I'm eager to get back to him."

Elizabeth cleared her throat. "I'm sure you want all of this to be over. I'm just not sure the new king is prepared to do what is necessary to protect you. Not like my sweet Atticus, that is. King Augustus was never truly prepared for his role," she commented. "His father never trained him properly. Atticus has been working beside his father since he could walk."

"Elizabeth, darling, your food is getting cold," Theodore chastised.

I gritted my teeth. "August will rise to the challenge," I said.

Theodore scoffed. "Atticus will help him like he always does." He stabbed his steak with his fork to accentuate his point. "Some men are born to rule. Some men are nothing more than puppets."

"Father," Atticus said. "Christine has had a trying few days."

Theodore ignored him. "I'm not saying anything she doesn't already know. Atticus is a man of his word. He sticks to his convictions." He looked at me. "Take you, for example. My son has known for years that he was going to marry you. He didn't let anything get in his way. A DuPont sees what he wants and does everything in his power to take it."

"Enough, Father," Atticus said, his tone lethal. "Christine is still adjusting."

I sat up in my seat. "Once Lord Nathan is captured, I *will* marry August. I don't need a man who tells me what to do. I crave equality. A *partner*. Your son might be ruthless and determined, but he refuses to listen to what I want."

A shadow of fierce emotion crossed Atticus's expression. His eyes darkened, his mouth curved down.

Theodore eyed me while cutting his steak. "I can see why you like her, son. A little push back can be fun."

"Don't talk about me as if I am not here," I spat.

"Christine holds affection for Augustus," Atticus said, his tone heavy as he stared at me. I watched him take a sip of his drink. "I didn't bring her here to convince her I'm the better choice. She's here because I want to keep her safe."

"She's here because that *boy* couldn't do the job," Theodore said. "Such a disappointment."

Atticus slammed his drink down on the table, making his wine spill over the rim. "Mother, Christine and I need to speak to Father in private. Would you mind enjoying the rest of your meal in your room?"

I'd expected his mother to argue, but to my utter shock, she smiled and nodded, as if getting told what to do was the norm for her. "Of course, son. You talk." She turned to me. "Come see me once you're settled. I can coordinate a spa day. Self-care is *so* important."

She grabbed a roll from the table and stood up, plopping some of it into her mouth. I'd always known Elizabeth DuPont was submissive in nature, but this was so odd to me.

Once she was out of the room, I turned to Atticus. "That was rude."

He replied, "What we need to discuss, she doesn't need to hear."

Theodore sighed. "You know I hate talking business at the dinner table."

"This is more of a family issue," Atticus replied. "It's about Augustus."

Theodore waved his hand. "What of him?"

Atticus gave me an apologetic look I couldn't decipher. "I think it's important Christine knows what we're up against. She wants to be included in things."

"It's so much easier when they aren't, son."

"Yes," Atticus replied, "but easier isn't necessarily better, now is it? Sometimes strength and defiance tastes sweet. That's why you pursued the queen twenty-two years ago."

My mouth dropped open. Theodore choked on the green beans in his mouth. He coughed a few times before responding to his son's accusation. "Excuse me?"

Atticus stood up. "It took me a while to figure it out. When the queen approached me two months ago with concerns for her son, I almost didn't believe it." He walked over to his father, a frown on his face. "You see, she wouldn't tell me who Augustus's real father was, so I had to do some digging."

"What are you talking about, Atticus?" I stammered, shocked by this turn of the conversation.

"The king found out that Augustus wasn't his legitimate heir. He was angry—rightfully so—and Queen Isabelle needed someone she could trust to take him out before word got out. I always thought it was strange she called *me*. I'm a DuPont heir, lethal in my own right. But she's asked you to do plenty of unsavory things over the years. You've always been close friends."

"*You* killed King Frederick?" I gasped, pressing my fingers to my lips while staring at Atticus. All of this was too much. I couldn't even process it. I thought coming to dinner with his parents was some sort of power move. I didn't realize Atticus would be telling me all of this.

"Atticus, that is enough," Theodore replied. His cheeks were red with anger and a hint of embarrassment. I could tell that his father wanted to end this conversation.

"Maybe even more than friends."

"You have no idea what you're meddling with," his father said.

Atticus didn't flinch. He glared at me with burning, reproachful eyes. "You want to be involved, Christine? I'll happily treat you like a partner. I'll tell you every dirty secret." He turned back to his father. "Tell me. Who else knows that you're King Augustus's father?"

Chapter Five

"This doesn't make sense," Christine said while rubbing her temples with the tips of her index fingers. "Explain."

My father looked like he wanted to leave, but I wouldn't let him get out of here easily. Our men might still report to him, but I was a force to be reckoned with.

"King Frederick isn't Augustus's father," I replied. "He is a DuPont."

"He's no bloody DuPont. That boy is spineless. You have no clue what you're talking about," my father argued, though I saw the way sweat collected on his brow.

"Isabelle came to me. She said that King Frederick

found out that Augustus wasn't his son. She was worried that they'd both be killed."

Christine shook her head. "No. That's impossible—"

I cut her off. "It is *very* possible. I'd arranged for King Frederick's death. It was no easy feat. We had to make it look like he died from natural causes and keep him isolated from everyone. I had twenty-four hours to pull it off. But you know what was strange, Christine? The timing of it all was very coincidental. Isabelle called me the night of my father's birthday party." I turned to face my father. "You were angry that Augustus was away on his yacht again."

"I don't have to explain myself to you," Theodore seethed. "That boy was wasting away every opportunity."

I glared at my father. "And you took it personally. Because it's your blood running through his veins. Frederick noticed. He confronted his wife about it and—"

"And she folded. She had me convinced no one would find out, but when she was questioned, she *failed.* That's the thing about strong women, Atticus. They never measure up when it counts. You can't trust them to keep their mouth or their legs closed."

"Shut up," Christine gritted. "I won't let you talk about her that way. Isabelle saved my life—"

"Who do you think helped cover up the murder, Christine?" my father asked. "Are you going to get down on your knees and thank me? I'm the real hero of this story." Christine flinched, and I wanted to kill my father for talking so openly about what had happened to her. She'd been harboring this secret for years, and now it felt like everyone knew. My father continued. "Frederick was sterile. He was going to leave Isabelle and try to knock up someone else. She needed a favor, and I was happy to oblige. In exchange, she helped us expand our empire."

"Isabelle told me August was in danger," Christine whispered. "She made it sound like the same people who killed King Frederick were after him."

"She lied," I said, my voice easy and direct. "Augustus *is* in danger, but not from me." I turned to my father. "Who else knew? Lord Nathan is building a rebellion."

"No one knew. And no one *will* know," my father insisted. "We're careful. Everything was taken care of."

"But you weren't careful," Christine argued. "King Frederick found out, and now August is in danger."

My father rolled his eyes. "Augustus had the world handed to him on a silver platter. If he can't figure it out, then he wasn't worthy of it in the first place."

I tugged at my collar. "Are you sure no one knows?"

"Positive. The only people that know are in this room or are in hell."

Pacing the room, I went over everything. Something wasn't adding up. It was possible Lord Nathan was spreading coincidental rumors, but I doubted it. He was too cocky. Too egotistical. Someone leaked Augustus's bloodline to him, and I needed to know who. Fast.

"You could always ask Lord Nathan yourself," my father said while leaning back in his chair. "How about instead of interrogating your father, you go out and eliminate the threat? I'm not the enemy here; it doesn't matter *who* knows as long as they're taken care of. I don't think we have anything to worry about."

I straightened my tie. "I just want us all to have the full story before I make my move. If Lord Nathan has information about our family, I want to be prepared."

"Does August know?" Christine asked softly.

My father answered before I could. "No. That idiot can't know. I don't trust him not to get high and tell the paparazzi. Goes to show you can have all the proper breeding, but it takes a firm hand to raise someone worthy of your name. Frederick ruined that boy. He could have had it all."

Christine shot up from her seat. "I've heard enough."

I watched her run out of the room as if it were on

fire, rage building within me with every inch of distance she put between us. I turned to my father. "We're not done."

He smirked at me. "Don't let that woman ruin you, Atticus. Don't let her spoil all our hard work. The ones that fight back are entertaining but not worth the effort. I've let you play your games because I think it's important to battle for what you want, but at the end of the day, I expect better of you."

I clenched my fists at my side. "I know exactly what you expect of me, Father," I snapped before fleeing the room after Christine.

Her bare feet padded across the hardwood floors, her long hair flowing behind her as she swiped at the stray tears falling down her cheeks. I'd been worried about this. It was too much. Too soon. I'd made her invincible, but it didn't stop the trauma from seeping in. It was like a tumor, growing slowly and taking over her soul.

"Christine!" I called as she ran to my bedroom and slammed the door shut. I reached for the handle and ripped it open just as she stopped in front of the window.

"You killed Frederick," she whispered while staring out at the castle in the distance. She was breathing heavily.

"I know you wanted to do it…"

She looked at me, her eyes glistening. "Tell me, Atticus…did you kill him for me or for August?"

I sighed. "The truth?"

"Always give me the truth," she replied.

"Both. I killed him for the woman I love," I said softly, while taking a step toward her. "And I killed him to protect my brother."

She shook her head in disbelief. "Atticus. All this time, you've been protecting all of us, haven't you?" Christine took a step toward me. "Rising up the ranks in your father's empire." Another step. "Making me stronger." She took another step. "Building August up…"

"August is infuriating and self-destructive," I snapped. He always had Christine's attention. He had everything handed to him. Was given a life away from the responsibilities of a DuPont.

"And yet you care for him," she whispered.

I reached out to tuck a fallen blonde hair behind her ear. "And yet I take care of anyone you love. I know you don't want to be here. You want to be with *him*."

"I want to be with all of you," she whispered.

And that was the damning thing of it all. She was greedy like me, not stopping until she had everything her heart desired. And she deserved all of it.

She didn't deserve Augustus right now, though. He had to man up. I had to let go. Leo had to step out of the shadows.

"Christine, I'm not the hero of this story," I whispered. I'd dreamed for years of having her look at me this way. Like I could save her. Like I'd finally measured up.

"I became my own hero, Atticus. I don't need someone to save me. I need someone to *love* me."

I grabbed the back of her head and slammed our lips together. She tasted like wine and divinity. Her sweeping tongue caressed my lips, begging me to open up to her. I crushed our bodies together and felt her dig the tips of her fingers into my chest. She moaned when I tugged at her silk pajama shirt, carefully unbuttoning it until her creamy skin was on full display.

I wanted nothing between us.

Her breasts spilled out of her pink silk bra, her rose buds poking through the thin material. I tore it off of her.

Christine moaned when I kissed her neck and shoulders and pushed her back against the windowsill. She wrapped her legs around my waist and let out a breathy sigh. Her lips were swollen and slick from our kisses. She rested her head back against the window and let her eyelids fall shut. I ran my fingers through her hair and savored the way her silky tresses slipped between my fingers. Christine gasped when I grabbed her ass and hauled her up higher. She let go of my waist and grabbed at my shoulders, digging her nails into my back. I growled into her lips and kissed her hard.

She forced my suit jacket off. Then pulled at my tie. I carried her to the bed and laid her down before unbuttoning my dress shirt as she slipped her shorts off. "Tell me," she whispered, fire flickering in her gaze. "Did he suffer?"

"You'd like that, wouldn't you?" I asked, noting how she pressed her thighs together, waiting to hear my answer.

Her fingers traced her dusty pink nipple. "I would." I watched her squirm, her thighs rubbing together as she tried to calm the ache between her legs.

Fuck. I knew she was perfect for me. This turned her on.

I nodded. "I made sure he felt every single ounce of pain." She dragged her hand down her stomach and slipped it over her mound. "I had to make it look natural," I said before kneeling at her feet. Christine was a queen. *My* queen. "So I found poison that wouldn't show up in an autopsy. But it's *very* painful."

She tilted her head back and pinched her nipple. "Did he cry?"

"Sobbed," I promised her. "Fat tears rolling down his cheeks."

She sighed as I pried her legs apart so I could see her glistening pussy. So perfect. So tight and pink and *wet*. I knew everything there was to know about Christine. But I wanted to lick every inch of her skin. Taste her. Take her so deep I was fucking her soul. I wanted to know what she looked like swollen with my baby. With bruised lips from *my* mouth. With red handprints on her ass from me.

I wanted her existence to be so intertwined with mine that my obsession with her allowed me to learn about myself.

"His body shook and trembled from the pain. He was writhing. And just before he died—" I paused to thrust my finger inside of her. Her gasp was music to my ears. "I looked him in the eye, and I said, 'This is for Christine.'"

I hooked my finger and caressed that deep need within her. She fucked my hand, grinding her needy clit against my palm while she imagined what I described. King Frederick begging for mercy. His weathered body shutting down.

"You're perfect, Little Monster. Perfect for me."

I started thrusting harder, watching her beautiful

body ride my hand. I had the world at my fingertips. She was chasing that high. Seeking relief.

I bit down on the tender skin of her inner thigh, and she fought to stay still. I raised my eyebrow and slipped another finger into her cunt. The muscles in her stomach tensed as she rocked her hips. The harder I pressed, the harder she rode my hand. I pressed my thumb against her clit, rubbing the pebbled nub. Her eyes fluttered, and I watched her lips part. I was giving her everything she needed. I would give her fucking *everything*.

My fingers.

My mouth.

My cock.

I fucked my fingers into her soaking wet pussy and kept rubbing her clit, milking every ounce of pleasure from her. Her body shuddered and shook, her muscles contracting. I kept my thumb planted on her clit, my fingers buried deep inside her.

"You know why I love you, Christine Abernathy?" I asked as she bit her lip. "You're not the perfect little rule follower. You demand your place. You claim." She wrapped her hand around my wrist and squeezed.

"Fuckkkk," she moaned.

Wet sounds filled the room. I could smell her sweet scent. Feel her squeezing my fingers.

"I love you because you want so much. You demand it all." Her pussy clenched around my fingers. Tighter. Gripping. Her thigh muscles tensed up.

"I'm dripping from your touch. You're perfect for me," she rasped.

I kissed her inner thigh as she caught her breath. "You're perfect for me, too."

Her eyes were like an ocean, full of depth and endless. I swam in them, floating above the murkiness, knowing that she could hold me up.

"If you don't turn off your phone, I will," she grunted.

Phone? I hadn't even heard it.

Once she mentioned the buzzing sound, I couldn't *stop* hearing it.

Bzzzz…bzzzzz…bzzzz

"I'm so close," she murmured.

I focused on her, watching her face twisted up.

Bzzzz…bzzzzz…bzzzz

"Who the fuck is calling?" she grunted.

No. No. We were so close. I just wanted to make her come. Just once. I'd earned it, damnit.

I kissed her and whispered, "Don't worry about it." I could smell my sweet girl drenched with sweat and sex. I kissed her neck and then teased her hard, wet nipple between my teeth. I wanted it to be good for her.

"It could be August." Her voice was husky and full of sex but also a hint of worry. Fucking Augustus. Always ruining things. I didn't want to let her go.

"I don't care about Augustus," I seethed.

My fingers reached for her once more, but she pulled away.

"But I *do*," she replied.

That was always the problem, wasn't it? I ignored her, then kissed her stomach. I was rewarded with a moan, the sound vibrating down to my cock. She was the fucking best. My monster. My fucking future wife. While I kissed her, I fucked my fingers into her. I then stared at her pink pussy that was covered in her sweet juices. I moved lower to lick her clit gently. She groaned and buried her hands in my hair.

Bzzz…bzzzzz…bzzzzz

The lusty haze in her eyes cleared, and she stiffened. "Atticus, you have to answer the phone."

"No, Little Monster. I want you to come for me."

She tugged at my hair, pulling me away. "Someone has called you at least six times. You should answer it."

I let out a curse. "I'll toss it out the window."

It wasn't fair. Something always got in the mother-fucking way.

"Answer the phone, Atticus. We have plenty of time."

I gave her one more look, wishing shit would settle so I could finally have the girl I wanted. I was tired of obsessing on the sidelines, giving her up for her own well-being. It was our time. It was my time.

"Fine," I snapped before looking for my discarded pants. I dug through the fabric until I found my phone and pulled it out. "Augustus," I groaned.

"He needs you," she whispered, regret lacing her tone.

"Yeah," I replied as my phone started vibrating again. "He always fucking needs me."

I stood up and shoved my pants on. "You can answer that here."

I glared at her. "And have you let him know you're alive? I'm smarter than that, Little Monster."

She scurried off the bed and followed after me as I made my way to the door. "Atticus. We don't have to do things this way. I can help. I can protect August, too."

I slammed the door behind me and turned the lock. She couldn't help me. I made her strong for *my* peace of mind. So she could heal. So she could be an unstoppable force. But I couldn't let her get hurt. I refused to let her get hurt again.

I'd already failed her once.

Once I was far enough away from her frustrated

screams and pounding on the door, I answered my phone. "What."

"I have Lord Nathan's best friend," Augustus said. "A man in an armored car is delivering him to you as we speak."

And when he hung up the phone, I let out a sigh. Of course he'd want me to do the heavy lifting. I had a long night of torture ahead of me.

But when I got back, her pleasure was *mine*.

Chapter Six

ATTICUS

Rupert Thames screamed like a bitch. He screamed when I sliced his heel. He screamed when I plunged a knife between his ribs. And he screamed when I smashed his hand with a mallet.

The man had no pride or sense of self-preservation.

I had the power to kill him. And he knew it.

"Please," he begged, his eyes watering with tears. "Please don't hurt me anymore." I felt no remorse. I only felt pleasure at hearing his screams.

"I'm going to kill your baby," I shouted at his face, "and then I'll kill you. And then I'll kill your mother and your wife. And then I'll kill your dog."

It wasn't hard to find out his weak spots. His wife liked to post the entirety of his life online, and even though I wouldn't call this pathetic excuse for a human a family man by any means, he didn't want his child to die.

Mostly because it would be a scandal that hurt his good name.

"Don't you *dare* touch them," he slurred.

"I'll do whatever is necessary to get the information I need," I breezed while wiping the blade of my knife on my pants. Splatters of blood coated my skin. I could taste the torture in the dense air.

He was angry now. I could tell by the way his lips were pulled back and his eyes screwed shut. He was desperate. He was pathetic. I had no intentions of killing an innocent baby, but half the battle was convincing him I *would*. "I don't know where he is," he lied.

Rupert Thames knew damn well where Lord Nathan was, and it was only a matter of time before he told me.

I cut him again. It was his leg. This time, he didn't scream. I supposed he was in too much pain for that. And the knife had hit an artery, because he was bleeding too much. I needed to move quickly or tie off his leg so he lived long enough to tell me what I needed to know. His blood seeped into the floor and mixed with the sweat of past victims in this very room.

"Tell me, is Lord Nathan worth dying for? How did he earn your loyalty? Are you lovers?"

His face screwed up in disgust, as if the idea of fucking another man was more grotesque than the torture I was inflicting on him. Men like him were so disgustingly repressed it was laughable. "No. Of course not."

"Is he blackmailing you?" I asked, and his eyes widened. "He is, isn't he? What's he got on you?"

Rupert shook his head.

"What does he have on you?" I asked again. "Give me a reason to let you live. Tell me." I was so close to breaking him. I could feel it. His eyes were pleading with mine. He wanted to tell me, but he couldn't. He just couldn't. I sighed. "If I walk out of here, then everyone you know and love will die. Perhaps I need to kill them in front of you?"

"It's not Lord Nathan I'm afraid of!" he roared. The man was so wired with agony that I could see veins popping in his forehead as his eyes rolled back.

Interesting. Was Lord Nathan working with some-one? "Explain."

He shook his head. "You might as well kill me. Kill everyone I love. We're as good as dead anyway."

I growled. Who the fuck was Lord Nathan working with? And why were they supposedly scarier than a DuPont? "Some things are worse than death, Rupert," I told him.

Blood from Rupert's nose covered his lips like war paint. The bright reds and oranges of the blood clashed with his skin. His eyes were green flecked with brown, scared like a deer in headlights. "A DuPont is worse than death," he said with a bitter laugh. He wasn't wrong. Rupert was breathing heavily, and I could hear his teeth grinding together.

He was already close to a mental breakdown. And I hadn't even started the actual torture.

"I guess you aren't a complete idiot," I said, moving to the other side of the table. I picked up a hammer and a small chisel from the table. "Tell me what I need to know, and I'll make it painless for you." I was lying. I would never make it painless. But maybe he didn't know that yet.

"I can't," he stammered.

"Alright then. I'm going to cut off your right hand," I told him. "And then I'm going to cut off your left hand…" I stalked over to him as he screamed a high-pitched sound like the squeak of a child.

"No, no, no," he bellowed. His eyes were screwed shut again, as if hiding his mind from me. But I saw it all. His fears. The damning realization that he was as good as dead. Tears streamed down his cheeks.

"I'm going to crush your balls in a vise, and then I'm going to cut off your left foot. And then I'm going to cut off your right foot. Then I'm going to cut off your ears." I lunged forward and started to dig my fingers into the soft flesh of his lobe.

"I'll tell you what I can!" he yelled, making me pull back. I wiped my hand on the front of my shirt as he steadied his breathing.

"Speak. I'm losing my patience."

"Nathan is building his army on the outskirts. He holds rallies in the towns with the most poverty. He announces the rallies a week before he arrives on a secret network. If you have a hacker, you'll find it easily."

I had plenty of hackers. Finding Lord Nathan was the original goal, but now I felt like there was more to the story. "Tell me what Lord Nathan knows."

He shook his head. "Lord Nathan is a pawn. The man you're really looking for is right under your nose, Atticus DuPont. You think you have this under control, but…"

His words slurred and his head bobbed.

Shit.

He was passing out. Torture was always a delicate

balance. You had to bring them to the edge without killing them so you could get the information you needed.

"Wake up!" I shouted before backhanding him. Rupert opened his eyes and shook his head, still not fully conscious. "What man is under my nose?"

Rupert shook his head, his eyes drifting closed. "The real threat is…" he murmured. "He's…"

His words were too soft for me to hear. Fuck, was he dying already? Had I tortured him to death? "Rupert," I said and shook him. "Don't die on me yet."

He gasped for air and his eyes opened, boring into mine. "You're being tricked," he whispered, saliva dripping down his chin. "Everything you know is a lie."

I leaned in close and rested my forehead against his. "What is a lie?" I asked. "Who is the real threat?" I grabbed his collar and shook him relentlessly.

His face was clouded with pain and terror. I wanted to know the truth, but it was too late. Rupert's eyes fluttered closed, and his face relaxed. His chest stopped rising and falling. His body slumped, turning to dead weight. I pulled back and stared at him in frustration. Fucking useless. I was better than this. I knew the delicate balance of life and death. I'd let my determination cloud my better judgment, and now he was dead.

He might have told me how to find Lord Nathan,

but I had nothing else. Just the smell of blood and death on my clothes and more questions than answers.

"You always were too eager," my father said at my back. I spun around, then glared at him.

"What are you doing here?"

He smirked. "Just reliving some memories. I remember the first time I brought you down here. You killed the rat before the fun could even start. There's an art to torture."

I gritted my teeth. Theodore DuPont was a ruthless bastard that made me the monster I am today. "He thinks Lord Nathan is working with someone."

My father stepped out of the shadows and poised himself under a hanging light. His fierce expression made me frown. "Of course he is," my father replied. "How else could he have gotten a bomb into the engagement party?"

It was an obvious answer. Someone high up was assisting Nathan. "That's what I'm thinking too."

"So who is he working with?" my father asked. "Did he tell you anything useful?"

I stared at my father. The question burned in my mind. Who would be smart enough to pull off something like this? The DuPonts were still at the top of the chain, but who would be stupid enough to take us on? "I don't know," I replied.

My father arched a brow. It bothered him when I didn't have answers. "Do you know how the DuPonts came into power, Atticus?"

I resisted the urge to roll my eyes. Of course I knew. He'd drilled our villain origin story into me a million times before. "Yes."

He messed with his cufflink. "We allied ourselves with the royal family. They gave us lucrative priorities with zoning and properties and turned a blind eye to our less than savory business decisions. It was disappointing to me when King Frederick learned the truth about his son—his legacy. We worked so very well together."

"We can still keep Augustus in power and maintain the same leverage we had before. We just need to get rid of Lord Nathan, first."

My father shrugged. "Lord Nathan is nothing. I'm not concerned about him, and I don't understand why you're so focused on finding him." He glared at me before continuing. "There will always be someone on the fringe who wants what we have. Everyone is looking for a new puppet now that King Frederick is out of the picture. And if things for our DuPont prince fail, then we will need to ally ourselves with the next people in power to maintain our position."

"What about Augustus?" I asked.

"What about him? If he isn't worthy of wearing the crown, the DuPonts will work with someone who is. I encouraged your friendship because I knew that you're the next generation. But at the end of the day, we survive. We *thrive*." He paused to stare at me. "But I suppose if you're determined to deal with Lord Nathan, you can go investigate."

I nodded. "Of course." The truth was out there, I just needed to find it.

He clicked his tongue and gestured at Rupert. "And clean that mess up before your mother sees. You know she doesn't have the stomach for our line of work." And with those words, he left the room.

I'd always known I couldn't trust my father. Eventually, I'd have to overthrow him. The only way out of this was with a crown on Augustus's head. I refused to work with anyone but him.

We just had to secure his position as king.

Chapter Seven

CHRISTINE

I was lying in bed, bored out of my mind, when Atticus came storming into my bedroom. Though it was dark, I still saw the splatters of blood on his skin. Could see the weight of the world bearing down on his broad shoulders. He glanced at me before walking into the bathroom. When I heard him turn on the water, I shoved the thick covers off of me and softly padded toward him.

"Where have you been?" I asked.

He stripped out of his shirt, and under the light in the bathroom, I saw gore painted across his neck, covering his tattoos as if the carnage was burned into his skin.

"Getting information," he replied before shoving his pants down over his hips. I leaned against the doorframe and watched him step under the steamy spray of water.

"What kind of information?" I asked as he lathered soap over his chest.

"The kind that doesn't really help me," he responded, scrubbing between his shoulder blades. He leaned forward, cupping his hands under the water, running it over his face. I watched him, my morbid curiosity peaking.

"What happened?" I asked.

"I just got done having a conversation with one of Lord Nathan's comrades."

I felt my body go cold. I wanted to be in that room. I had some answers I wanted, too.

"What did you talk about?" I asked, but my voice was small.

"He gave me riddles and a half-assed solution to finding Lord Nathan. I have a hacker working on it now and should have an answer within the hour. I'll be leaving soon," he finally said after he'd rinsed his face. He turned the water off and stepped out, wrapping a fluffy towel around his middle before moving to the sink.

"Leaving?" I croaked. "I want to come with you."

"No."

He scrubbed his hands down his face before turning to look at me. "Atticus. What am I supposed to do? Just wait here until you return?"

He walked past me toward his closet, and after throwing on some sweats and a shirt, he grabbed a duffel bag and started shoving clothes inside of it. "That's exactly what I expect you to do."

"Atticus. I don't want to just wait here," I said, whining.

He tilted his head to the side and looked at me. The look on his face told me he was done with the conversation. "This is what you're going to do. You are going to get your ass in that bed and sleep."

"But—"

"No buts, Christine. Get in the bed!" he yelled, making me flinch. I felt tears well up in my eyes.

"You can't just order me around like this," I finally said.

"I can't trust anyone not on my payroll. I think this might be bigger than we thought, and I need to know that you're safe, okay? I need to go, and I need you to stay here. Do you understand?"

I shook my head. "I don't feel safe here, trapped with your men."

His shoulders dipped in defeat. "I trust them, though. You're safe with them."

"I don't want to be safe. I want to fight." I turned and stormed from the closet.

"Christine." He sounded exasperated and I hated him for being so stubborn. What use was making me into a monster if he didn't trust me to protect myself?

I heard him call my name as he followed me, but I ignored him. I didn't stop until I threw myself on the bed with a thud. Covering my face with the pillow, I tried to block out the world around me. I could hear him hovering, knew that he was waiting. He touched my back, and I jerked away, rolling to face him. The look on his face sent my heart into overdrive.

"I'm sorry. I'm sorry," he said, slowly touching my arm. "I'm sorry, Little Monster."

I wasn't sure why, but I was crying. The tears just kept coming. I felt helpless. I wanted to run, to fight, to scream, to do anything but just sit here waiting for him to fight my battles for me. "I hate this. All of this. And I'm starting to hate you, too."

Atticus had always made me feel capable and in charge. But I hated that he was just like every other man in my life. Trying to control me. Trying to keep me up high on a pedestal of blood and destruction.

"I can handle your hate if it keeps you safe," he murmured.

I sat up and leaned closer to him. "Please, don't leave me," I whispered as I leaned into his body, pressing my wet cheek against his stomach. He wrapped an arm around my shoulders and held me close, but I could feel his pulse racing under my fingertips.

"I'll be back soon, I promise."

"If you leave, I'll run. I won't stay here," I said, my voice breaking as I clung to him.

He didn't say anything. Despite the fact that he held me as close as he could, I could see that he was fighting with himself internally. He wanted to tell me to stay here, but he didn't. I felt his heart pounding as if it were trying to hammer its way from his chest. He kissed the top of my head and squeezed me before pulling away.

"Tell me something, Atticus," I whispered while peering up at him. "Why turn me into a killer if you won't trust that I'm capable?"

He reached for my cheek. "The goal was never to make you a killer, Little Monster. The goal was to make you stop fearing the world."

"And yet, here we are." I let out a bitter laugh. "You're the scared one now."

"In some ways, you're right," he said without an

ounce of regret. "*And* you're wrong. I was never afraid of the world. I'm just afraid of losing you."

He kissed me quickly before pulling away. He hurriedly packed the rest of his things. I felt like a fool. I'd let myself believe that we were having some connection, that something was growing inside of my soul, and I was sure that he felt the same. I touched my chest lightly and felt the pounding in my heart. It was a connection of a different sort. A confusing, volatile connection that I didn't understand at all.

"Why don't you stay with me tonight?" I asked. "We never got to finish what we started."

He gave me a solemn look. "Augustus is waiting for me. Bastard's been on a rampage ever since…"

I scowled. "Ever since you lied to him. Ever since I *fake died?*"

He strapped a gun to his hip and tugged on his shirt. "I'm not going to apologize for protecting either of you. Augustus needs to stay focused and take down Lord Nathan. Now he has the proper incentive. We both know he won't do anything for his own sake. But he sure as hell will burn the world down for you."

A spike of insecurity rushed through me. "You really think so?" My question was barely a whisper. I couldn't help but think about the years Augustus *didn't* fight for me. I didn't blame him, nor did I harbor any regrets. I needed to leave, and he needed to stay far away from me. Far away from all of this.

"Of course. Christine, he might be a pain in the ass and definitely doesn't deserve you, but the boy *loves* you. Do you think otherwise?"

I bit my lip and looked away. I loved August, but I didn't trust him to love me back. This was all still so new, so fresh. I was tired of being guarded. I wanted to be free. "I don't know," I said.

Atticus waited for me to look back at him. I did, and he was right there, standing right in front of me. He placed his hands on my shoulders, and I felt the electricity spark between us. "Augustus never stopped loving you, Little Monster. He was devastated when you left, and he's been a mess ever since…"

I swallowed and looked away. "Is it wrong that I'm glad?" I whispered, looking at the floor. "It makes his feelings more…real. I must be a terrible person. I don't want him to think I'm dead. I don't want to be cooped up in this tower while you fight my battles."

"Christine," he said, his voice low and sexy. He leaned closer to me and kissed my ear, his warm breath causing goose bumps to rush over my skin. "There is nothing wrong with wanting us to love you back. With wanting that love to feel tangible. You can admit all the things you want, and I'll do everything in my power to give them to you. As long as it doesn't compromise your safety."

"I know what I want," I said, licking my lips. "I know what I need, but…"

I trailed off, unsure if I should dare say what was on my mind. He waited, and I finally decided to finish my thoughts. "I don't know that I'll ever be enough for all of you."

Atticus let out a roar and grabbed me, pushing me down until I was lying on the bed. He climbed on top of me, his lips twisting into a mischievous grin. "I don't know why you need reassurance or what more I can do to convince you that I'm on board with whatever you desire. But when all is said and done, you will have it all, Little Monster. I didn't fight the ranks of this empire just to give you a mediocre existence. Augustus and Leo will join us even if I have to tie them to your wrists or beat them into submission. You understand?"

I nodded, unsure what to say. Something about his words sounded like a threat. "Okay," I replied, my voice barely above a whisper. "Will Leo come to see me while you're gone?" I asked.

A shadow crossed his face. "If you wish."

"Will you hurry back?"

Atticus grimaced and kissed me again. He got up

and walked to the door. "I'll be back before you know it."

I watched him leave, wondering if he really believed his own words. I thought about the things I'd seen, the things I'd done. The danger being a part of this world could be. I'd seen countless people torn down and discarded, draped with cobwebs and left to decay in the shadows. There was no guarantee that I wouldn't be another forgotten casualty left to rot.

I stayed in my room for a few more hours, unable to keep my mind off Atticus. I needed something to keep me busy. I kept thinking back to his promises and his words. I had to get out of this room. I might have been the only prisoner here, but I'd have rather been in a cage with a hundred chains than alone in his bed, smelling his sheets, wearing his button-up shirt.

I got up and grabbed my shoes, then threw a cloak around my shoulders and opened the door. I was surprised to find no one on guard outside. I was even more surprised to find that I had free rein of the rooms on the floor. I took a few turns, running down halls and climbing stairs. Aside from my quick dinner with his parents, I'd not had time to take in the tower. It was huge. It was stunning.

It was the kind of place only a psychopath could love. There was no warmth or personal effects. It was masculine but looked like it belonged on the cover of a magazine, not somewhere someone lived and breathed. It was cold and harsh. Just like Atticus.

Being alone without a guard felt like a trick. The moving cameras overhead were a stark reminder that I was never alone. Atticus probably instructed everyone to give me the illusion of privacy, despite the cage he'd locked me in.

I finally stopped in front of a large arched window that towered tall in the room. I touched my fingers to the cool glass and sighed. I felt trapped. This was all so confusing.

"Hello, darling. Atticus said you might be out and about."

Elizabeth DuPont stood smiling, with her fingers tangled in front of her. The morning light cast a halo around her head. She was truly angelic. "I was wondering if you'd like to spend some time together today."

I opened my mouth, not sure how I was going to tell this woman I was in no mood to socialize, but she held her hand up, forcing me to stop talking. "I contemplated manicures or having my stylist visit, but then I realized you probably didn't want to do any of that. But I think I found *something* that you'll enjoy. Follow me, darling."

And with those words, she spun on her heels and started walking down the hall. I let out a shaky breath before following after her.

I didn't trust this woman. Every second I spent with her made my skin crawl. She was too perfect, and I wasn't sure if she was genuinely friendly or if she was more calculating than I realized. I was under Atticus's thumb. I had no choice but to trust him. But I still couldn't shake the feeling that Elizabeth was neither friend nor foe—just a brutal pawn in this game.

She led me to a plain door that seemed to have no purpose or reason. She opened it and I walked inside. I stood there, stunned and silent. Tears instantly sprung to my eyes. No…no way…

I closed my eyes. I opened them again, just to make sure I wasn't dreaming.

It was *glorious.* A full-size training room with mats, workout equipment, and a punching bag. It was all state of the art, and a few men were grappling on the ground, letting out loud grunts as they wrestled. "You seemed like you needed to let off some steam," she said with a shrug while beaming at me.

I had a feeling she was pleased with my response. I ran my hand over a rack of weights while she observed me. "Thank you. I've been needing…"

"We all have our outlets, darling," she said with a coy smile. The posh woman looked out of place in this room meant for sweat and skill. Her skin glistened and the diamond studs in her ears shone brightly under the fluorescent lights.

"What's your outlet?" I asked, curious about her. A shadow crossed her features, the look unexpected but hauntingly familiar.

"I'll let you in on a secret, Christine," she said, her eyes clouded with sadness. "I might be a DuPont, but I'm trapped in this game just like you. Just like everyone else."

My chest tightened, and I felt suffocated. This beautiful woman could be telling the truth. She could be just as trapped as I was. I swallowed and took a steadying breath. "I don't believe that. I don't believe I'm trapped here. I will get out."

Her eyes twinkled, and she looked almost like she wanted to laugh. "The heart has chains, even if you can't see them. You can *feel* them."

A strange breeze rushed over me and I shivered. I felt like I was in the presence of something dark and deadly.

"You never answered my question," I finally replied.

"Pain," she replied, her voice as dry as the desert. "Pain is my outlet. Something my husband is incredibly skilled at. Is that too dark for you?"

I swallowed, unsure how to respond. She was a woman who reminded me of an angel with her features, but she moved like the devil. She was fascinating. And I wanted to know more. "No," I said softly. I understood her probably more than I wanted to. It's why I punched the brick walls until my knuckles bled. "I get it."

Her smile was chilling in its authenticity. "I'm glad you understand."

And just like that, she left me alone in the gym.

Chapter Eight

CHRISTINE

I slammed my fist into the punching bag without a glove, reveling in the feel of my knuckles burning from the impact. Sweat dripped down my cheek and onto my lip. I licked it away, salty aggression blooming on my tongue. The taste of frustration was suffocating me.

The DuPont men let me out of my prison cell and allowed me to train. However, I wasn't given any knives or guns. I supposed they had been made aware of just how lethal I was.

I preferred it that way.

I'd been working out with only my fists since the sun

came up, in an attempt to exhaust my body and my mind.

When I was training, I didn't think about August or Leo. I didn't think about Lord Nathan and the bombs. Isabelle's body.

I thought about nothing. I let my body do the thinking for me. I let my mind freeze over into a stagnant nothingness of biting pain. The moment I started thinking, was the moment I started feeling, and I didn't want to feel anything for a little while.

Not with Atticus pushing me away.

Not with August thinking I was dead.

Not with Leo betraying me.

I pulled my arm back and slammed it forward, the bag swinging back and forth with the force. I took deep breaths, the air burning my lungs, heightening my senses and tingling my skin. I only stopped when I heard a voice behind me.

"Nice hit," a weathered tone ricocheted around the room. I spun around and stared in shock at the old man responsible for making me a killing machine. Hudson wore a black jogging suit, his face drawn and tired, like he'd been out running for days. His eyes were filled with the knowledge of war and life, but they had a dullness to them that made it feel as if he hadn't slept in a decade.

He was tall and imposing, always towering over me. Skinny, but his muscles rippled with each inhale. He kept his hair short and clean cut. His right cheek bore the scar I'd put there two years ago.

"I should have known you'd show up, considering Atticus is your boss and everything," I said, my words dripping with resentment.

He strolled over to me without a care in the world. I massaged my knuckles as he leaned over the punching bag, almost touching it with his nose. I watched as he deeply inhaled. Hudson always loved the smell of sweat. It made me uncomfortable when we first met, but I'd gotten used to it.

"Are you angry?" The old man's voice was gruff and filled with gravel, a slight rasping sound every time he spoke. He liked it when I was angry. Loved how it fueled my fighting spirit and made me work harder to draw blood.

"No," I replied, happy to disappoint him. I liked Hudson—before I knew he was sent to train me by Atticus—but I wasn't in the mood for his mind games today. "Why are you here?"

"Why do you think?" he retorted, straightening his spine and putting his hands on his hips. I was almost sorry I asked.

"I think you're here to remind me I'm a weapon,

just like you did three years ago." I shrugged, then flexed my biceps, the sleeves of my hoodie hugging my arms. I kept my eyes trained on him, noticing how the lights reflected off the light stubble on his chin, dancing across the wrinkles in his forehead.

"No. I'm here to remind you that you can use this anger. That you *should* use this anger." He was calm and casual, but something in his voice made me think he was trying to trick me. His lips twisted into a snarl as he pointed at the punching bag. "Why waste time hitting this when you could do something much more satisfying?"

Something about Hudson always put me on edge. I knew I was skilled. My trauma forced me to overcome, and I had a penchant for causing death. However, Hudson was skilled at getting inside of my head. He knew my weaknesses and made me want to tear my body apart. His methods were cruel and demanding. Sure, I was the best at what I did, but with Hudson, I resembled a child with a gun in her hand and no sense of restraint. He made me mindless and dangerous. I was thankful for the man, and before I realized he was hired by Atticus, I cared for him.

Now I just viewed him as another tool used to control me.

"I don't trust you. You've been bought and paid for by the DuPonts. You're their bitch," I said bitterly.

He laughed, a cackling sound that doubled as a chuckle. "Oh, that isn't entirely true. I'm here to help. But I guess you're right, though. You shouldn't trust me."

He always wanted to help. Or at least his version of it.

"You want to fight, Hudson?" I asked while rolling my neck. I was exhausted and feeling cagey.

"Would it make you feel better? You always were easier to talk to after I let you hit me a couple of times."

I scoffed. It was near impossible to hit Hudson. He was too good. Even in his old age. If I was in a better mood after our sparring sessions, it was only because I was shocked that I'd gotten a few punches in. "Fine."

I watched as he curled his fists. The old man's hands were large, callous and rough, fingers stiff and sticking out at odd angles, knuckles like a boxer's.

He struck first. He *always* struck first. His curled fist landed on my stomach, knocking the air out of me. "You're always so eager to hit me," I coughed out. "One of these days, I'll be ready for it."

His fist struck my jaw, but I blocked another punch to my throat with my arm. He continued on a series of quick punches, and I blocked them. Our sparring matches were always a game of cat and mouse until I figured out a way to draw blood. One thing I liked about Hudson was that he never held back. He didn't treat me like the weaker sex. I once asked him why he was so brutal with me, and he'd said something that still stuck with me. *"Your enemies won't be, so why should I?"*

"If I don't hit first, then I get hit," he chuckled, jumping back and giving me a moment to recover. "My face is too pretty for bruises."

"You're an ugly bastard and you know it," I scoffed, forcing myself not to smile. I had a unique relationship with the old man, one built on a foundation of insults and pain.

I surged forward and kicked him in the ribs. The asshole didn't even flinch. "Kick like you mean it, kid."

"I don't want to knock you out of commission, old man," I replied with a laugh before punching him in the jaw.

Pain bloomed on my bruised knuckles, and it felt like home.

He grunted more words. "You're strong, stronger than you were when you left." I hadn't been practicing as much, but I was fueled by my resentment of the Crown and all this pent up frustration. "I know why you're angry," he said, while dodging another hit.

"Oh, yeah?"

"You're angry because Atticus isn't treating you like the capable woman you are."

Hudson had never called me capable. He preferred to train me with insults, breaking me down so he could build me back up with grit and blood. His words caught me off guard, and he took the opportunity to punch me in the stomach again.

I sputtered and choked down the burning pain. "We're not here to talk about Atticus. We're here to fight."

My knuckles turned red, and fleshy purple swells appeared with specks of blood.

"Fine then," he said, his fist striking my jaw once more. It was getting harder for me to block him. "Let's fight."

He landed a hit to my ribs.

"You aren't getting any good hits," I said, my voice strained. He was still in good shape, and it took more out of me to block his punches than it did to punch him.

"You're a terrible liar," he said, right before he punched me in the mouth, causing a slight trickle of blood to run down my chin.

The old man had trained me in every way possible. I'd worked hard, learning hand-to-hand combat, weapon training, and the art of stealth. He'd taught me everything from how to slit a throat from behind to how to seduce a man to get him to do whatever I want. At first I hated it. I hated every minute of it. It felt like a betrayal of who I used to be. But then I learned to *love* the power.

We battled for hours. The room filled with sounds of crunching fists smashing into flesh and bone. The pain was a symphony of cracking and bending. I was out of breath and pissed off. The DuPont guards watched with their mouths hanging open in surprise, some of them hissing in secondhand pain when Hudson landed a kidney punch.

None of them stopped us, though. Probably because the bastards were too scared to intervene. They had taken away my knives and my favorite handgun, so I was forced to use my fists and my feet. The men were smart. They knew what they had a hold of. A human weapon. One that didn't need bullets, only knives and anger.

Hudson and I didn't talk. We only fought. The more I was hit, the better I felt. I had a quick temper, and I needed to release it.

Once, my anger was terrifying. It was a fearsome animal, perched on my chest, clawing its talons into my ribs in a blinding, hot panic. Now, I welcomed my fury.

I used it to my advantage. Hudson taught me how to tame the beast and make it work for me.

Our sparring session went on for a while.

I got in a few punches.

Hudson hit me in the face, in the stomach, and in the ribs.

My face and torso were covered in bruises.

He was bruised and bleeding as well.

I hadn't been this happy in a while.

"You're getting distracted," Hudson said, breaking me out of my thoughts.

I looked at my hands. My knuckles were bleeding, but that was normal.

"You always do that," he continued. "You get all lovey dovey over your bruises."

I rolled my eyes, which was probably not a good idea considering the way my vision blurred.

"I like seeing them. They remind me how strong I am," I replied while I lunged at him, this time landing on the balls of my feet, twisting my ankle. My foot slipped on the slick mat, and I fell, my hands planted on the ground to catch myself. Hudson landed on top of me, his elbows framing my head and his hands resting on the mats beside me. My arms were trapped beneath me.

"You get careless when you're emotional," he grunted.

I struggled to move beneath him, and I knew I only had a few seconds before he'd take full advantage of my position. I twisted my body, trying to wrench my arms away. A slap to my ear made my head ring, and I gritted my teeth. "I'm not emotional!"

"Prove it. Get me off of you."

Hudson had taught me how to survive a fight. He'd taught me a lot of things that I hoped I'd never need. But now, I was grateful he'd forced me to learn. If I didn't have the skills, I'd be dead.

I turned my head, trying to bite his hand, but he was too smart. He moved it out of the way before I could sink my teeth into his flesh. His other hand reached for my throat.

I caught his wrist in both hands. "That's it. You're fighting back," he hissed, his breath hot on my neck as he moved his thumbs to my throat, pinning me to the ground. I struggled to breathe while I kicked him, but it was no use. "You're angry because you aren't in control of your own life," he shouted. "You're angry because you should be in charge, not Atticus."

I closed my eyes as he continued to lecture me. "Why are you telling me this?" I grunted.

He squeezed tighter. "Because you need to understand it if you're going to get away from the DuPonts."

I wriggled in his hold, trying to break free, but I knew it wasn't going to happen. He wanted me to fight back, but I knew I didn't stand a chance against him. He was too powerful, too smart. So I did the only thing that I could. I jerked his hands off my neck and pulled them close to my mouth.

I bit his wrist, sinking my teeth into his flesh.

His hand loosened, but he didn't let go.

"That's it," he hissed, his hot breath brushing against my ear. "Fight back. Fight for your freedom."

I dug deep within my reserve of strength and threw him off of me, slamming him into the mat with every muscle clenched.

Hudson was shocked.

I was shocked.

My heart thumped and adrenaline took over. I had to finish him off. I had to win.

Thinking quickly, I jumped on top of him, sinking my fingers into his arm, digging my nails into his skin. I was ready to kill him. I wanted to. I needed to. "That's it!" he encouraged, as if I wasn't drawing blood. He twisted his body and pushed me off him, sending me flying across the mats and into the safety wall. It shook violently, rattling the metal frame. "I'm impressed," he said, his eyes full of excitement and pride.

I wiped at the blood dripping down my face. "Again," I said before charging after him.

Hours later, when my legs wobbled from exhaustion, Hudson yelled, "Enough." He was always the one to end our fighting sessions, and usually only when I was on the verge of blacking out. I wiped the sweat from my brow and drank from a water bottle. I offered Hudson a drink, but he declined. Ruthless bastard ran on whiskey and pain.

As I sat on the floor and tried to catch my breath, he stared at me. "What?" I asked, knowing he was itching to say something.

He cleared his throat, his wrinkly face a portrait of anticipation. "I'll probably get in trouble for this, but I'm getting old and tired of working for the DuPonts." He wiped at a bead of sweat on his temple.

I eyed the guards in the training room but didn't stop Hudson from speaking. "What?"

"You shouldn't be locked up in this tower. You worked hard to protect yourself, kid. You earned the right to make decisions for yourself."

I chewed on my lip, surprised. "I thought you listened to everything the DuPonts told you to do. It's why you spent three years training me."

"Don't sound so bitter. It's not becoming of a lady," he teased, "*or* a future queen."

I scoffed. "Didn't you hear? I'm dead."

"Even ghosts still haunt. But you can't do anything trapped in this gilded cage."

He was right. This was a cage. I loved Atticus and was thankful for all he'd done to protect us, but I hated that he was so controlling.

"So, what do you suggest?"

He leaned back on the mat and stared at the ceiling. "I trained you to be competent, Christine. I taught you how to fight back. If you want out, then leave. We both know you could if you really wanted to. The only person holding you back is *you*."

I stared at him, my mind working the words over. He was right. I'd trained and killed my way out of a lot of bad situations. It was time I used the skills I'd honed to free myself. "Thank you, Hudson." I stood up, wanting to hug him but knowing he'd be too proud to take my gratitude.

"Whatever you do, do it for yourself, kid. Don't be the girl that lets the rest of the world control you. We both worked hard to give you independence."

A question fluttered across my mind, one I was scared to know the answer to, but needed all the same.

"Was any of it real?" I asked. "Us? Our friendship?" For some reason, I needed to know. Atticus had controlled so much of my life behind the scenes that it was impossible to recognize what was real. Was I even alive?

He sighed. "When I was first sent to Harvington to train some Lady of the Court, I was less than thrilled. I almost didn't take the job," he admitted. "Told Atticus I'd take a look at you and see if you were worth my time."

I nodded, half expecting this. "And?"

"Some people shut down when they're hurt. *You* got angry. I saw you throwing punches with no direction and decided you deserved to feel strong again." The words ripped open a wound I'd been keeping closed for a long time. "I wasn't your friend, Christine. I'll never be your friend. I was Atticus's pawn, and you were his precious project."

The words stung, but I couldn't deny them. "I'm sorry he forced you to work with me." I didn't know what else to say.

"You're a survivor. I respected that. Respect is far more valuable than friendship." He stood up and rubbed his knuckles. "And as long as Atticus views you as something he can claim, he'll never respect you. Go show him that you're a force of your own. You'll both be better for it."

My stomach knotted. I was so conflicted. Hudson had been my instructor and mentor. I'd trusted him. I'd respected him. And I'd loved him like a father, but now I realized he'd never loved me back. I was a job.

But he respected me, and he was right. In this world, respect was far more precious than friendship or love. I considered his words and then left the room. I had no doubt I could escape DuPont tower. It was only a matter of strategy. So I started planning my escape.

Chapter Nine

Augustus was biting his fist in the seat beside me, glaring out the window, like Lord Nathan was hiding behind every tree and shrub. The seat of the car was cold and hard, grounding me.

"Can we fucking drive faster?" he asked, making the driver accelerate. The anger simmering in his veins was palpable and toxic. I was relieved to see him taking a hands-on approach, but was still apprehensive about how long this would last.

The grief would catch up to him eventually. And when it did, he'd be self-destructive again. I just hoped he could get the job done first. We had to take down Lord Nathan.

Augustus looked regal and deadly. He'd worn a black suit fit for mourning and had at least showered since the last time I'd seen him, but it didn't hide his turmoil. His face was pale and his eyes were bloodshot and weary. He crossed his arms over his chest and wore a dour expression. Each of his movements was surprisingly deliberate and calculated. When I'd greeted Augustus this morning, he stood with complete confidence, like a man ready for war.

I didn't have much else to do but observe my brother while we drove through the countryside. We would have taken the jet, but wanted to be discreet.

"What will we do when we get there?" I asked. I had a town car full of men following behind us and a pistol holstered to my hip.

"Kill him," Augustus answered, his tone commanding and merciless, like a bomb exploding in my face. His face was hard and his tone was dead serious. It didn't give me the sense that he was looking forward to the killing, but that he was prepared to do what needed to be done. He truly seemed to be eager to rid the world of our enemy in a swift and lethal fashion.

"Is that what you really want?" I asked. I didn't know if that was the best course of action. We needed to know what Lord Nathan knew—and who else he'd told. Augustus was in danger, but I wasn't sure if the timing was right to tell him about his lineage. He was volatile under the best of circumstances, but the man sitting beside me was completely unhinged. *And untrustworthy.*

"You're the one who told me to step up and get my hands dirty."

I sighed. "You're more than welcome to kill the fucker—after I've had the chance to question him. I just want to make sure we're smart about this. We don't know how many men he has or if there would be backlash."

"Who gives a shit about backlash?" Augustus snarled. He was getting agitated again. I could tell by the way he uncrossed his hands and clenched his fists in his lap.

"You should." I had to remind him of our position and how precarious it was. "You're the king. People will take sides. Some will side with you, while others will side with whomever they feel looks stronger. Our enemies need to fear us, and our allies need to respect us. Who knows how this will affect the rest of your reign? It's wise to be cautious, at least for now."

Augustus huffed, his cheeks puffing up. "*Our* enemies? Since when are we on the same team? I'm the king. You're a criminal." His eyes narrowed as he looked at me.

I chewed on the inside of my lip. We became members of the same team the day he was born. "We've been working together for years. Sometimes because our parents forced us together, sometimes because you *needed* the skills and connections the DuPonts have. But we became a solid team the day this psychopath murdered the woman we love. So stop acting like I'm against you and lean on me. All good rulers use every resource at their disposal. I'm your best shot and you know it."

"How can you stay calm?" he croaked, his face turning pale from the pain. His nails dug into the seat, and the leather hissed. "I can barely think straight. Barely get out of bed. I'm starting to think you never loved her at all. Not the real her anyway. Because if you did, you'd be as fucked up as I am." The lines on his face were deep, a mask of sorrow and loss, not of strength and wisdom.

"I loved her just as much as you did. Maybe more. We just show it in different ways," I gritted. I *was* grieving. I was mourning a dream—I mourned hope for a life with her where she didn't hate me for controlling her. "I'm not sure how to process what happened. How to accept the fact that she's gone." I shook my head and clenched my teeth, the lie like acid on my tongue. Augustus stared at me. "Don't think for a second I don't want to rip every limb from his body and watch him bleed out. I'm just saying…be smart about this," I reiterated, unsure if he heard me the first time. "You don't need to rush in and kill him, because he's not worth the risk of putting us in danger. Use the element of surprise, catch him off guard, incapacitate him before killing him. We need to make sure we have all of our bases covered, just in case. Do you even know how to use a gun?"

"I have no fucking clue what I'm doing!" He let out a frustrated growl. His breath practically smelled like sulfur. I could feel the heat from it, like I was in the presence of a volcano about to erupt. "I've never killed anyone. I don't know how to lead a fucking kingdom, and I certainly don't know how to avenge her death. I just have to do fucking *something*, or I'll lose my goddamn mind. Sitting here is killing me. Being in that castle that smells like smoke is brutal. And you know what, Atticus? I finally get it now. I know how she felt when she walked through those castle doors. How she hated everything about that place because it reminded her of her trauma. I put her there, Atticus. I did. And she *died* there."

I pinched the bridge of my nose, refusing to look at

him. I couldn't handle the sympathy he was forcing on me.

"I'm the reason she died," he choked out between dry sobs. "The reason she suffered. I'm a fucking murderer. She was safe in Harvington."

I bolted upright, my gut reaction to punch the shit out of him and beat the shit out of me. "This is not your fault," I said, trying to make my point. "You didn't make those fucking bombs go off."

He sighed, his voice cracking. "I took her to that hell, Atticus. I put her through shit."

"It's not your fault." I wasn't sure how many more times I'd have to repeat those words to him. I wasn't sure how many more times I'd have to convince him.

"It is. It's all on me." He wrinkled his brow. I was stunned speechless. My tongue twisted at the taste of bile in my throat. "I miss her," he said. The tears that had built inside started to burn their way out. He bowed his head, his fingers stuffed into his mouth so I wouldn't hear him sob. The sounds of his cries were muted, like a television blaring beyond a closed door. When he sat back up to speak again, the broken look on his face was jarring. "Three years, Atticus. Three years I missed her, but it never felt permanent. Now, I'll never get her back, and it *kills* me." He punched the tops of his thighs. "I need a minute to think. Park the car!" he commanded the driver.

The stunned guard driving our car pulled off to the side of the road, along a stretch of winding highway where we hadn't yet seen a house or sign of civilization. He got out and started pacing, thrusting his hands through his hair as tears streamed down his cheeks.

We didn't need this right now. Augustus needed to be angry. Detached.

Lethal.

I got out of the car and stared at him. "Man up. You can't break down right now. We have a job to do."

"Man up? Man up? I can't. I can't do this," he said while walking a line in the grass.

I opened my mouth to say something cruel—something to get him pissed off enough to pull himself together. But he shocked me once again.

He charged after me and wrapped his arms around my body, pressing his face into my neck. "I can't do this. It hurts too fucking much." The ache in my chest made it hard to talk.

I didn't hug him back, and he didn't seem to mind that I didn't return the sentiment. I was numb and confused. Augustus and I had always kept each other at a distance. I cared for him. I protected him because I had to. But I wasn't good with emotions and I wasn't good with *him*. I didn't know how to support Augustus other than tearing him down.

I stood there, rigid, for minutes. He didn't seem to care what I did. I couldn't tell if he was waiting for some kind of signal from me that I was okay with his outburst. He was willing to put up with my silence.

But after a while, it became too much. I felt his sorrow and it was strangling me. "This isn't the time to cry," I snarled while pulling away. "We have to kill this guy."

"Who the fuck are you to tell me what to do? You're not my friend. You're not my brother. You're not my father. You're just some guy I know who follows me around and does what I say."

"I'm just trying to help you pull yourself together."

"Don't forget you failed her just as much as I did," he said through clenched teeth, his airway opened, but the words were muffled, just like his sobs had been.

"I didn't." The words escaped me before I could censor myself.

"You saw her last. You let her slip through your fingers. *You* should be standing here sobbing like an idiot."

"Shut the fuck up," I said. I stepped toward him. I could have punched him right then and there, but I didn't. Throwing a fist at him would have been too easy.

"You have no fucking idea what I've been going through. You don't know the regret. You don't know the guilt. You're so busy, wrapped up in your own shit, that you haven't seen what I've been going through."

"Sorry for not sending you fucking flowers, Atticus."

The car full of guards watched their king lose control.

My body was tight. I'd never been at a loss for words, but I was choked up, the lump in my throat so large I couldn't swallow. Augustus being vulnerable cracked me wide open, and I didn't know how to process it.

But it was time to be cruel. It was the only way. He wiped his nose on his sleeve, and I rolled my eyes. I couldn't let him lose focus. I had to make him stronger. "You know the difference between us, Augustus? You break when things get hard. I get *harder.* I become invincible. If you're going to legitimately lead this kingdom, you need to be level-headed. You need to be resilient. Enduring this pain is what makes you stronger." I glared at him. "She's gone."

"I know."

"She's dead."

"Fuck, I know."He shook his head and wiped his eyes with the back of his hand. "It's all I think about. I wake up and it's all I remember. And when I sleep again, it's all I dream about. What the fuck am I supposed to do?" He twisted his head from side to side in distress.

"Quit being a pussy. You're going to get us both killed if you're not careful. Get angry, Augustus. Get pure fucking livid. It will give you the motivation you need to take down Lord Nathan."

"I can't do it," he said, his voice cracking.

"You can. You just need to understand the reason he has to die."

"I already know the reason."

"Tell me."

"He killed her."

"Say it like you fucking mean it!" I screamed, the veins in my neck bulging.

"He killed her!" he roared with equal power. "He murdered her. He killed *both of them*. My mother is dead and so is the woman I love, because of him."

I nodded. If only it were that simple. That wasn't the only reason we had to take him down. Lord Nathan threatened both Augustus and Christine. As long as he lived, he was a danger. Christine might be alive now, but I couldn't take the risk that he actually succeeded in killing the woman I loved. The lies felt like weights on my chest, but it was the only way. "He's the reason we'll never have her back. We can't have her alive—that was taken from us—but we can have her death. That is the best we can do. We can have revenge. And we will."

"Fine," Augustus said while rolling his shoulders back. "I'll do it."

"If you're sure," I said, eyeing him suspiciously. He nodded. "We'll have to be careful though. I'm sure he's still on the defensive, so I don't know when the best time is to strike, but we'll take the first opportunity we can." As much as I wanted to walk through Lord Nathan's front door and put a bullet in his skull, we had to be delicate. Augustus couldn't know about his lineage or Christine.

"I'm sorry," he said.

I frowned. Augustus never apologized for anything. "What for?"

"For not being the man I'm supposed to be. For"—he paused to gesture between us—"breaking down like this."

The lump in my throat grew. "Do better," I replied. I could have coddled him, but it wasn't in my nature to tell someone what they wanted to hear. "For Christine."

He nodded. "For Christine."

Chapter Ten

Atticus had not returned. It was so frustrating not knowing when he would return or what he was doing. The anger and worry I felt killed me. I might be able to help him if he were to include me in what was happening.

What if he was in danger?

What if Lord Nathan got to August?

I paced the floors of my pretty prison cell. The guard outside my door coughed, reminding me that I wasn't alone, I was never alone. My plan for escaping was in its early stages, but most of it involved killing every man in this building.

But what about Atticus?

I closed my eyes and tried to relax. Maybe it was time to stop being okay with being a pawn. Maybe I'd just start kicking over the chessboard until I ended up moving on my own terms.

A sharp knock on the door startled me. I turned around and watched it slowly open. Theodore DuPont looked me up and down, his eyes like slugs against my skin. I returned his perusal, not wanting to be intimidated by Atticus's father, especially now that I knew what kind of man he was. Theodore DuPont was tall, his shoulders broad. He looked like his son but greasier somehow. More crooked. His spine curved unnaturally. His eyes were dark, cold and distant. His skin was slick, like his eyes, a strange symbiosis of body and soul. He looked greedy and worrisome.

I tipped my chin up. "What are you doing here?"

"You have a visitor," he said mockingly with a wave of his hand.

I bit the inside of my cheek, trying to control my anger. I walked over to him and leaned on the wall beside the door. "I don't want to see anyone. Where is Atticus?" I hissed.

"Atticus is away on business and I'm in charge. You're *my* guest, Lady Abernathy," he said as he stepped into the room and closed the door.

"I don't want to speak to you," I said.

"My son has always had a soft spot for you. I've never understood it." Theodore's voice was a venomous rasp, snakes hissing in a warning.

He licked his lips, and his eyes roamed my body. I didn't appreciate the way he looked at me. He reminded me too much of Lord Geralt, and it made me sick to my stomach.

He reached out to brush his finger along my shoulder. Theodore's hands were small, but callous; knobby knuckles lined his fingers in a grid of scars.

"Don't fucking touch me," I said.

He snapped his hand back. "I don't understand why my son is determined to comply with your whims. The handsome royal guard waiting downstairs looks like a man in love. I hear whispers that you juggle the attention of many. Tell me, where does my son rank in your heart? Is he just someone powerful to use? Are you like Isabelle in that regard? She raised you, after all." His eyes glinted as they met mine.

I took a step back, stunned. I'd been certain he was just a mean man, not a mean *and* angry one. He was the vicious kind, the kind that said things just to see your reaction.

"Don't talk about her that way," I shouted. Leo was here? I needed to get away from Theodore DuPont and talk to him.

"Isabelle used her body to get what she wanted. From King Frederick. From *me*. I can see that you have certainly inherited that skill. You've had your hands in many men's pockets. Perhaps that's why my son is loyal to you. Why King Augustus wants to *marry* you. You're a whore."

My face flushed red with anger; I was going to kill the man. "You know nothing."

He surged forward. He was breathing heavily. I could see his chest move, and the pulse in his neck beat like a drum. "I know *everything*. My son gets the job done and that's why I put up with his exploits. You are nothing more than a stepping stone to power. I know firsthand how beneficial it is to fuck a queen, so I let my son do what he wishes." His body odor wafted off of him in greasy waves like rancid meat. "But if you start to become a distraction, I know how to kill you. I trained with Hudson, Christine. I know your weak points." I looked into his dark eyes and saw a cold, deadly resolve. He was dead serious.

As I pinned my lips shut, he continued. "Take your cues from Isabelle. When all of this is done, use your body to seal the deal with a king. We have big plans for you and the future king. Deals to be made. And if my son, the king, or even that sorry, love-sick guard can't keep you satisfied, let me know. I'll be waiting in the wings." The words spilled out of his mouth like an oil leak.

"You're insane," I said.

He smiled. His pitiless eyes were as hard and cold as steel. "I'm an opportunist. Just like you. Just like my son."

I turned my back to him. "What do you want?" I asked.

"I want you to know that you are my guest at the moment, but if you start acting sour or if you decide to run, I will use you up like the whore you are." He leaned into my ear. "You're nothing in *my* kingdom."

He slithered away and I waited until the door closed to let the tears well up in my eyes. One of the guards had definitely told him what Hudson had instructed me to do, and he wanted to make sure I stayed put.

Was Atticus with me so he could use me?

I didn't want to believe it, but if this kingdom had taught me anything, it was that you couldn't trust anyone.

Theodore's threat burned itself into my brain.

Everything I knew felt like a lie, and even if Theodore was just trying to fuck with me, it didn't stop the doubts from spilling through the cracks of my resolve. Was I using these men? Were they using me? Was I a whore for loving all of them? Needing them?

My head was beginning to spin and my heart felt heavy, like a thousand pounds of cement poured in my chest. Thoughts and questions swirled around me in an ever-tightening spiral until I felt completely enveloped by the unknown.

I had to get out of there. I had to think. I grabbed my bag and started to make my way toward the door, but then I stopped. Fear consumed me. It was such a strange emotion—one I'd refused to feel long ago. It was as if Theodore knew how to rip a timeless scab from my heart and relished in the sight of my heart bleeding at his feet.

I heard a noise outside the door and wiped my eyes. I was a prisoner, but I wouldn't let anyone see me break. Leo was here. He'd know what to do. I glanced in the mirror and smoothed my hair.

The door opened and Leo entered. He looked tired. His blond hair was disheveled, and his face was covered in stubble. When our eyes met, I felt my soul shiver with anticipation. We stood silent, locked in anticipation as he dragged his green eyes up and down my body, lingering on the bandages on my arm, the bruises forming on my skin from my sparring with Hudson, and the scrapes on my knuckles.

"He said you weren't hurt," Leo finally choked out.

I looked down at my hand and shook my head. "I was burned a little but also was training."

He took a cautious step toward me. "This isn't training, Christine," he said before carefully reaching for my hand and stroking my knuckles. "You're hurting yourself. *You're always hurting yourself.*" He had whispered the last part of his statement, as if he couldn't handle the truth of it.

I shrugged and pulled my hand back, wrapping it in my opposite one. "I have to become stronger. Hudson —the man who taught me how to fight—showed up."

We stood, me in a defensive stance and him looking down at my hands, his face concerned. "Did he hurt you?" Leo asked, his tone low and dangerous.

"I did some damage to him, too," I answered, trying to lighten the mood.

He let out a shuddery breath and smiled, relief washing over his face. He straightened and crossed his arms. "I'm glad you're okay."

"I'm not." At my words, his eyebrows pulled together inquisitively. "What are you doing here?" I asked, taking another step to put some distance between us. "How did you find out I was alive?"

"I knew the first night. Was checking security footage." His answer made my stomach drop.

"And yet you haven't told August what Atticus is

doing," I replied, suddenly remembering whose side Leo was really on.

He nodded. "I'm not your enemy." He looked into my eyes, and his face softened. "I care about you, Christine." He placed his hand on my cheek. "I'm worried about you."

I slapped him away. "If you were truly worried about me, you wouldn't let Atticus keep me locked up here."

"You can't go back to the castle, Christine. It's not safe."

A bitter laugh escaped my lips. "You sound just like Atticus. I don't need you to protect me, Leo."

He frowned at my response. "I'm not trying to protect you. I'm trying to *help* you."

I stepped back. "By keeping me away from August?"

He shook his head. "By keeping you out of the crossfire when Augustus does something stupid. When Lord Nathan attacks—again. When more people lose their lives in a stupid war you don't need to be in the middle of."

I crossed my arms and looked down. "I can help. I'm capable, Leo. This isn't right."

"You shouldn't have to help. You should be in Harvington where it's safe!"

I threw my hands up in frustration, wincing at my stiff muscles. "This again? I'm not leaving, Leo! I'm in too deep. I feel too much. Tell me, who do you serve, Atticus or August? You sound like you've switched sides."

He closed the distance between us. I placed my fingers on his chest, planning to push him away, but he was warm. His heart was racing. "I've only ever been on *your* side, Christine." My lips parted, but I couldn't speak. His body felt liquid against mine, like he was on fire. His face moved closer. "I care about you more than I should. You're my friend. I don't want to see you hurt. Why can't you understand that?"

The word *friend* was a harsh reminder of the distance between us.

I looked up into his green eyes and saw pain. He was trying to save me. He was trying to protect me from the cruelty of Aldrich. Suddenly, I felt my indifference reignite and my rationalizations rush back. How could I trust someone who thought locking me away was okay?

"What do you want?" I swallowed. "What do you *really* want, Leo?" Maybe if he could tell me the truth, I'd understand him more. There was always so much distance between us. His duty. My title. August. Atticus.

"I want you to be safe." My fingertips traced his

jawline. I could feel his breath as it hit my face with every word.

"What else?" I asked while breathing him in.

"I want…" He licked his lips while staring at my mouth.

"You want?"

"I want…" he whispered against my lips. He closed his eyes and tensed. His lips were just touching mine, and he pulled back. "I want you to be happy. I want you to be safe."

"What about what *I* want, Leo?" I asked.

He lifted his hand to my face, his fingertips lightly touching my cheek, before cupping the back of my head. "Tell me," he groaned.

"You," I whispered. "I want you, and I want my freedom." His lips touched mine, gently at first, then harder, his tongue licking the top of my mouth. I wrapped my arms around his neck and kissed him back, his taste sweet in my mouth. Our lips collided like two people drowning. He forced his mouth against mine, and I wanted him more than anything I'd wanted in a very long time.

The smell of Leo's cologne was intoxicating, a spicy musk, the type that made your body tingle and your head spin. "Fuck, I've wanted this for so long," he admitted between kisses. Leo tasted like freshly baked bread with a hint of salt from the ocean breeze.

His tongue pushed into my mouth, hot and furious, the assault delicious, and I worshiped him. Kissing Leo felt like closure. Like acceptance. My body melted against his. Leo's hands swept over my back, grazing the nape of my neck, making shivers travel up my spine.

We kissed at the center of possibilities, my lips drilling holes into his soul, his breath a caress of sunshine on my face, his touch coaxing the blood flowing through my veins. I placed my hands on his cheeks and saw fire in his mouth as he kissed me again. I wrapped my arms around him and held him close, too close for any enemy to touch. He touched me selflessly, as if I was on fire.

He said my name.

He said my name as he kissed me.

He said my name as he took my breath.

He pulled away, and I was left swaying in his arms, my head spinning. I opened my eyes, and he was looking down at me with a look I had never seen before.

My heart swelled with a new kind of hope.

"Let's go, now," I said while clutching his shirt. "Let's leave here. We can do this, Leo. Tell August I'm alive and—"

Leo squeezed his eyes shut and let out a groan. "August?"

I narrowed my eyes. "Yes. We need to go to August—"

One word was like a knife slicing through us.

"You're *using* me. How could I be so fucking stupid?"

My hooded eyes widened, the daze dissipating. "What?"

"This isn't real," he said while taking a step back, his fists clenched. "This is just a game to you." His words stung. I was left speechless, my eyes swollen and wet. Leo stepped back again, his eyes full of hurt. "Let's just forget this ever happened."

I shook my head at him, desperate to tell him the truth. "Leo, can't you see that—"

"You're trying to escape to Augustus."

"I'm not," I argued. "This is real."

"It's not," he rasped. "You don't see me as anything more than a way out of here. This is a trick. Why should I believe you?" he asked, his voice barely a whisper. His face looked pained.

"That's not true," I said, my voice shaking.

"You're not the Christine I knew. Stay here," he said while turning around and walking away. "I'm not taking you back. You might not love me, but I love you. I don't agree with Atticus on a lot of things, but I do want to keep you safe. No matter what it takes."

"But I do—"

He held his hand up to stop me from finishing my statement. "Don't lie to me. The Crown is cruel, but you've never been. It's hard to look at you when you act like *them*."

He walked out of the room with those damning words.

I let out a cry of frustration and dropped to my knees. I buried my face in my hands and waited for the tears to subside.

A part of me wanted to run after him and beg for him to understand me. But Theodore's words were still heavy in my mind.

Maybe he was right. Maybe I used these men. Maybe I was the whore he accused me of being.

Chapter Eleven

ATTICUS

I was tired of sitting beside Augustus in a cheap hotel in Redview, outside of the city. Lord Nathan was supposed to be running a rally in the square tonight, and waiting was killing us both.

When Augustus wasn't pacing the floors or demanding something of someone, he stared out the window, looking lost and determined all at once.

"Three fucking days of waiting here," he growled to himself. I knew just how long it had been. Every fucking tick of the clock was a reminder that Christine was locked up in the DuPont tower with my father. I knew Hudson and Leo would take care of her, but that didn't make being away any easier. Leo had been sending one word messages to me since the night they'd visited, withholding details about their reunion in a way that made me suspect it didn't go as well as he planned.

I shouldn't be happy about that, but I was.

"We can approach him tonight," I said.

"I'm going to make Leo come here," Augustus gritted while pulling out his cell phone. "I know he needed a personal day, but it's bullshit that he's off grieving while we're doing all this work."

I bit my tongue to stop myself from telling Augustus to leave him be. Leo was doing an important job right now, watching over Christine and making sure she's safe in my empire. I knew my men were loyal, but the longer I was away, the more restless they got.

We'd sent the royal guards away once we'd realized they drew too much attention. A collection of suits in this small town was likely to start gossip, and we couldn't afford to give up our position. It was predictable that Lord Nathan picked townships on the outskirts of the kingdom to rally in. He was bolstering the forgotten members of the kingdom and handing them loaded guns.

Just as Augustus's fingers touched the surface of his phone, someone knocked on the door. We were in a hotel that played host to a lot of the city's criminals.

We'd chosen it honestly because the building was run by a man who owed me a favor.

Augustus froze, staring at the door.

"It could be anyone," I said, ducking back behind the scarlet flowered quilts that served as our only window dressing, "or no one. Stay calm."

The knock sounded again, and I watched with a sinking feeling as Augustus stood up and walked around the bed to the door. He put his ear to it, taking a moment to listen. I pulled my gun from the waistband of my pants and aimed it at the ground, ready to shoot.

"What do you want?" Augustus asked more loudly than he intended. He took a deep breath and tried again, his voice a little smoother. "Who is it?"

"It's the cleaning staff. Just wanted to make sure everything was alright in there."

I was about to tell Augustus to let them in when the door opened and a foot slipped in first. It was a girl, but that was all I could tell from where I was standing.

Augustus stepped back, letting the girl in and closing the door behind her.

"Should I clean out here or in the bathroom?" she asked.

"Just the bed and the floor," he said, rubbing a hand over his hair and stepping back. "Leave the rest until later."

The girl stepped further into the room, and a smattering of dim light drifted into the far corners. I recognized her immediately.

"Eva?" I said, emerging from behind the curtain to look at her. "What are you doing here?"

Eva was a daughter of one of my father's associates and was probably more bloodthirsty than I was. At barely seventeen, she was lethal and resourceful. A perfect yet deadly combination in our line of work. Eva was pale and dark-haired, with a smattering of freckles across the bridge of her nose. She wore all black, a long-sleeved shirt, pants, and a pair of combat boots. "Your father sent me. Said you might need some assistance from someone less…recognizable." She then bowed to Augustus. "Hello, Your Majesty."

"Your father sent a teen?" the moody king scoffed. "What are you going to do? Cyberbully Lord Nathan?"

Eva's face was impassive as she looked down at Augustus. "I'll likely do more than you," she replied. "Do you even know how to form a fist?"

Augustus turned red. "You little—"

"Enough, Eva." I didn't like that my father sent her. Either he was trying to spy on me or he gave her a job separate from my own responsibilities.

Eva ran her hand through her hair, and the curls bounced like springs as she started to pick at a thread on her cuff. "I'm here to help. Either you can let me do my job or…"

"Fine," I snapped. I didn't want to listen to whatever threats she had. Ultimately, the only person Eva was loyal to was her family, and her parents clung to the old ways of the DuPont organization—specifically *my* father.

"This is ridiculous," Augustus said. "I'm calling Leo."

My brother then stalked out into the hallway, his phone pressed to his ear. The moment Eva and I were alone, I scowled at her. "Why are you really here?"

"Your father wants me to see Lord Nathan's army. Get some inside information on the bastard. He's heard rumors. Apparently, your little trick with the future queen wasn't convincing enough. Lord Nathan is still going on about finding her and marrying her."

"Fucking hell," I said while running my hand through my hair. "Someone on the inside must be leaking information. We need to interrogate everyone at the tower."

"I'm here to keep an eye on the situation," Eva replied.

"Why didn't my father call me? Does he not trust me?"

"Can you blame him? You've gone crazy for that

girl. No one trusts you to think straight where she's involved," she replied with a teenage dramatic roll of her eyes.

I looked at the door and lowered my voice. "How is she…"

"Who?" she asked, her dark eyes twinkling.

"You *know* who," I snapped.

"Oh. Lady Abernathy? She's good, I suppose. Training with Hudson. By the way, how'd you pull that off? I've been begging him for years to work with me."

I sighed. Hudson was probably beating her black and blue. It always bothered me to see her like that. Their training was brutal and vicious. I had to force myself not to kill him when I saw he'd broken her finger.

"Don't mention her to King Augustus," I warned.

"Duh," she replied just as the door handle twisted, indicating that Augustus was coming back inside.

"Leo will meet us there tonight," he said, scrolling uneasily through his phone. "He sounded pathetic. Wish he would pull himself together."

The irony in Augustus's statement was not lost on me. Just a few days ago, he was sobbing in a field and hugging me like his life depended on it. Between Eva, Augustus, and me, I was sure half the town knew we were there by now. "We might have to change locations again. I don't want to sit here while rumors spread. Maybe show up to the rally later."

"No," Eva said, folding her arms across her chest. "You need to stay here. That's how we'll get to Lord Nathan. He'll show up. People from all over are coming to this thing. Looks like a Renaissance fair outside. No one will think twice about two men staying here for the rally."

Augustus and I looked at each other. "You're right," I said after a moment, my eyes meeting his in agreement. "We need to stay here. He'll show up, we just have to be patient."

"I hate this bloody town," Eva murmured. "It's been a hell-hole ever since the rebellion three years ago. I heard they had so many bodies they had to burn them in mass graves."

I scratched my chin, searching my memories. "Wasn't Lord Geralt involved in that?" I asked.

Eva scoffed. "My father says everyone blamed Lord Finich, but Lord Geralt led the army behind the massacre. Pretty ironic that his brother is now here pretending to save the day and offer them vengeance on a silver platter."

Augustus and I exchanged a look. Maybe this was a weakness we could exploit later to turn his militia against him.

The next few hours were a series of back-and-forths between Eva, Augustus, and me. No one wanted to agree with any of the plans brought up. Eva was ruthless and cared nothing for me or the king. She was here for a job, casualties be damned.

Another knock landed on the door. "Must be Leo. Let's hope he's more help than the teenage mutant here," Augustus scoffed.

When the king opened the door, Leo was out of breath and staring wide eyed at the room. My heart clenched when his gaze landed on me.

"Atticus, we need to talk," he said, his words like an automatic weapon.

Augustus scowled. "You're *my* guard; what could you possibly need to discuss with Atticus? We've been here for days while you—"

"Atticus. It's important," he insisted while staring at me. He had that wild look of determination and frantic worry. I looked at him and saw a man plagued with indecision. I could see the sadness, apprehension, and horror in his eyes. His hands betrayed him as they trembled at his side.

"What the hell is wrong with you, Leo?" Augustus spat.

Leo looked at his king and bowed slightly, though the respect was rushed.

"I just…I need to speak to Atticus."

"Just spit it out already," Augustus yelled, commanding him.

I pushed myself off the wall and stalked over to Leo, determination in every stride. I knew in my gut that something was terribly wrong. When I tried to shove past Augustus, he balled his fist and rooted his feet to the ground, stopping me.

"Tell me what's going on," Augustus sneered.

"Not right now," I snapped before looking at Leo. "What's wrong?"

The wary guard's eyes fluttered between Augustus and me. I realized immediately it had to do with Christine. He wouldn't be this secretive otherwise.

I shoved past Augustus, nearly knocking him to the floor and making Eva laugh. "Men," she snickered condescendingly as I followed Leo into the hall.

Augustus followed closely behind, not willing to let us get away without learning what was going on. "Both of you stop right now and tell me what's going on!"

I paused to pinch the bridge of my nose in annoyance.

Leo gave me an apologetic look, his eyes heavy. His eyes stared at me, chest rising and falling as each breath was drawn in through his nose. "Christine escaped DuPont tower. No one can find her."

His words were damning. My nose picked up the musky scent of fear clinging to Leo's skin. Augustus clutched his chest and nearly fell over. "This is a cruel joke. Why would you say something like that?"

I ignored my brother to glare at Leo. "What do you mean she escaped?"

The air around Leo's body was frigid, his skin cold to the touch. His lips pressed into a thin line as he struggled to form the words he wanted to say. "There's a pile of bodies left behind. She's gone, Atticus. *Gone.*"

"What is he talking about?" Augustus rasped. "Tell me the truth, Atticus."

The pain in my chest was almost unbearable. I fought the urge to collapse to my knees, crumple like a child.

The world spun, the floor rising to meet my face. My body ached in every place where I knew Christine had touched. My mind flashed with her wild golden hair and the hateful eyes she flashed at me the last time we'd spoken.

She was gone.

Gone.

Gone.

Gone.

"What happened? What's going—"

My fingers squeezed a part of myself for comfort, and my mind went blank as the world faded away.

"Atticus," Leo said, his voice rough. "Atticus, you have to help me find her."

I didn't respond. The prickly feeling at my neck was like needles burrowing in my veins.

I looked at Augustus, who wore an expression, an odd combination of relief, anger, and concern. "She's alive?" he whispered so softly I almost didn't hear him.

Leo cleared his throat, answering for me when my throat closed up. "She's alive. For now. And we need to fucking find her."

I didn't move. I didn't want to hear anything else. A coldness started in my legs, burning like ice at the thought of losing her. "Yes, Augustus. She's alive," I said again.

"For now," Leo reminded me once again.

"Why?" my brother croaked. "Why would you let me think she was dead?"

He looked at Leo, then back at me. "Because she was safer dead," I said, forcing my nerves to settle and the cold no-nonsense attitude to echo in my words. "Because she was safer with me."

"Obviously not," Augustus bellowed. "She's out there now. Alone."

He grabbed the collar of my shirt, and I allowed it

only because I knew the rage he was feeling was mostly my fault. I'd let him believe the woman he loved was dead. I waited for a moment as he swelled with fury. I swallowed just as he reared his right fist back and slammed it into my cheek.

My head snapped to the side, the pain instantly stretching across my face. My lips twisted into a smirk before I pulled my own right fist back and punched him in the jaw. I'd wanted to do this for ages. Augustus had always stolen her attention. Had always thought he had a right to her body—her soul. And she might be gone now, but I would find her. I would keep her. She was mine to cry over. Mine to miss. Mine to *love*.

When he staggered, I brought my knee up and slammed it into his lower stomach. I brought my right fist down again and again, the sound of flesh against flesh echoing through the hallway.

He slammed his fist into the wall beside me, caving the drywall in and making me jump back. He growled and pulled me down by my shirt. A sickening thud echoed through the empty hall as his forearm collided with my shoulder. I clenched my teeth to keep from crying out as Augustus shoved me against the wall.

He pressed into me, his angry eyes boring a hole into mine. I wiped the blood from my lip and spit it into his face. He pinned me against the drywall. "Right now,

I'm going to find Christine," he said, his tone deadly. "So I don't have time to fucking end you for being a lying, scheming prick. But once she is safe in my bed, you're done."

He released me with a hard shove, sending me into the wall with surprising strength. I exhaled, my head hitting the wall with an audible thud. I had told myself to keep my emotions separate and hidden. If I was going to be the leader of the DuPont empire, I had to be cold.

But all I could feel was sick.

Christine.

If she was out there, then she was in danger.

"Let's go," I said, my voice broken and weak.

The two of them were already headed down the hall toward the exit by the time I pulled myself off the wall. Eva exited the room and gave me a dirty look as I passed, her eyes narrowed in disgust.

"You're letting them get in the way of your job," she said to me, her voice low and hard. "I understand staying close to the king, but this girl isn't worth your time."

I paused. "You stay here. Be safe, Eva. I know everyone in our world treats you like an adult, but you're still a kid. Observe and report back."

She rolled her eyes, her signature look. "Fine. I'll do

the job you're incapable of doing," she breezed. "Chase after that worthless king of yours."

I didn't respond, just walked out the door.

My heart was beating rapidly in my chest, and my face was hot from the pressure, which was starting to tear me apart. There was a small, muted sense of pride blooming within me. My Little Monster had escaped a tower I'd attempted to flee many times over.

But I would find her again.

And I'd spank her ass for leaving me.

Chapter Twelve

CHRISTINE

Blood soaked the stone floors, a crimson pool mixed with a gray ooze that bubbled and made sucking sounds as it cooled on the cold stone tiles. The air was thick with the stench of burning flesh and death, mixed with the acrid smoke and ash of discharged weapons. The wound gurgled wetly as I pulled the blade from the man's throat, a faint whimper escaping his lips before he fell silent once more. I dropped the DuPont guard, and he landed on the ground with a thud, the life fleeing his brown eyes as he bled out.

The air was stale and stunk of sweat, shit, piss and blood. The knife I'd stolen from Hudson was duller than I would have liked. It was made of steel, with a handle of white bone. The blade itself was dark and oily black, and the blood on it was the color of dried fruits, like plums or figs.

I could hear boots pounding on the tile floor, so I quickly continued my escape. I'd tried my best not to take too many lives, something that I couldn't think about too much as I ran.

I didn't want to disappoint Atticus.

I didn't want to feel trapped.

But I couldn't stay here. I didn't trust Theodore. Something was off about him, and the longer I stayed here, the more in danger I was.

I turned the corner and almost hit a man who had a Thompson SMG in his hands and a look of surprise on his face. I grabbed hold of his collar and flung him into the long row of paintings that lined the hallway. His finger was tightening on the trigger when the machine gun bucked in his hand, sending a long burst of bullets toward a window that had already been blown out from when I tossed one of my earlier attackers out of it.

"I don't want to kill you, but I need to take that gun so I can get out of here," I gritted. The man's face was filled with fear, his eyes wide and pupils dilated. He was gaunt and his skin was a mixture of oil, sweat and grime. His hair was dark and curly, a slick of dirt that covered his scalp and fell into his eyes.

He shook his head. "Mr. DuPont will kill me," he stuttered.

"Looks like you die either way," I replied. "You can either give me the gun and give yourself a head start or die now. I've already proven how far I'm willing to go to escape."

He paled. Obviously, I could take the gun from him if I wanted, but I was giving him a choice. I struggled with not wanting to hurt Atticus's empire while also wanting to be free. "Okay," he whispered before handing me the gun. His breath was hot and heavy like a furnace, but sour with bile.

"Good," I replied. I watched the man crumple to the ground, fear making him collapse. My right hand held the machine gun, the warmth of its barrel a pulse on my palm. My left hand felt along the cart's wall, mapping it through the vibrations and impact of my fingertips. "I'm going to run. I suggest you do, too," I replied before stepping past him and jogging down the hallway.

My goal was to get someone who had the emergency passcode to the elevator. When I first escaped, the building went on immediate lockdown. I tried to get a guard to open the elevator for me, but he didn't have the bypass code. Apparently, it was something only a DuPont had access to.

I just had to find another way.

My heart was pounding in my chest as I began to hear gunshots, screams and shouts.

"She went that way!"

I kept running and was thankful that I was running in the direction of the staircase that I'd seen when going to the training room every day. I didn't know if it led anywhere, but I certainly wasn't going to wait around here like a sitting duck.

I heard a door open behind me and stopped running, sliding to a halt and taking a few deep breaths.

My heart beat once.

Twice.

Three times.

Boots scurried away from me, and I breathed a sigh of relief.

I had to steady myself and prepare myself before I took another step. I could see far enough to know that the staircase was empty. I sighed in relief. I took a deep breath and gripped the gun in my hand. I could feel its weight and the smoothness of the handle.

I was safe for the moment, but that wouldn't last long.

I could feel the cool air against my warm skin. My

muscles twitched on the trigger, my fingers playing out their death dance.

I took one step and then another. The air in DuPont tower smelled of wealth and luxury, but was tinged by the smell of gunpowder and burning. The carpeted staircase led down to a black marble floor. A grand crystal chandelier hung from the ceiling, filling the space with a rainbow glow. The corridor was all white and gold, a luxurious and expensive aesthetic.

I looked around, my ears straining to detect any sound.

I could see a pair of red-tipped shoes sticking out from behind a gold statue. I took a step closer, seeing a designer silk skirt and hands that clutched at a white blouse. The eyes that stared up at me were wide and full of fear.

"D-don't hurt me," she whispered, her voice choked and strained.

"Elizabeth?" I said. Elizabeth looked like a frightened deer. Her eyes were wide and terrified. She was shaking and her hands were held up in a submissive pose, as if she were pleading for mercy. Her clothes were disheveled and haphazard, pulled on in a hurry. For someone who raised her son to take on a criminal empire, she sure seemed frightened, as if she wasn't used to the sound of guns going off and men gasping for their last breath.

I knelt down beside her, feeling her body trembling as I listened to the sound of boots approaching. There was a large, long wooden desk that sat before the entrance to the grand dining room, so I dragged her behind it.

"Don't make a sound," I whispered while aiming the gun at her. I was embarrassed and ashamed to use her this way, but I was still in the DuPont penthouse and I needed elevator access to get to the ground floor and get out of here.

She nodded, her face blotchy with tears as I hid us from the men who were running down the hallway. I leaned over her, checking to make sure that they hadn't seen us. There were two men in gray uniforms, with black bulletproof vests, both boldly wearing the family crest of DuPont printed on the chest.

"Why are you doing this? My Atticus loves you." Elizabeth was wearing a light floral perfume. Her fear was like a sharp blade in my nostrils; I could feel the shape of it, smell its caustic odor.

I eyed her. The truth was, I loved him too. But I was tired of men locking me up and telling me what to do, and I definitely didn't trust Theodore. I'd caught him lingering in the training room. Regardless of my feelings for Atticus at the moment, his father couldn't be trusted. I wasn't going to stay here any longer.

"Shhh," I hissed, my head on a swivel. The men started running down the hall.

"I just don't understand," she cried.

I looked at her, feeling sorry. In a brief moment, I allowed myself to think that I could have been Elizabeth. If I hadn't fought for my life. Terrified of the world. Controlled by a powerful man claiming to love me. If I allowed everyone to dictate my life, then I'd end up just like her. Kind. Complacent. Obedient.

Atticus claimed to love my monsters, but his actions proved otherwise. I was ready to prove him wrong. I grabbed her arm.

Atticus's mother's voice was choked, tears staining her face. "Don't hurt me."

"Take me to the elevator. You're going to let me leave, and I won't hurt you." I softened my tone. "I don't want to hurt you, Mrs. DuPont. But I need to leave."

"Okay," she hiccupped. "But don't you think you should talk to Atticus? Where will you go? What will you do?"

I hadn't exactly figured out my plan once I got out of here. I wanted to find August and tell him I was alive, but also felt nervous about going back to the castle. Atticus was right, it was too dangerous. If I had my way, I'd grab all three of them and leave this kingdom for good.

"I don't know. I just can't stay here." She nodded, and the haunted look in her eyes made me cock my head in curiosity. "Mrs. DuPont…do you…do you want to go with me?"

She flinched, her eyes wide with wonder as she absorbed my question. "Me? Leave?" A shadow crossed her expression. "No, sweetheart. It's too late for me to leave." The robotic way she spoke sent shivers down my spine. "But come along, if you're determined to leave, then I suppose I'll help you. You better hold that gun to my head so my husband doesn't punish me for this."

My brows raised, but I did as she asked, following her toward the elevator doors while positioning the barrel of my gun at the back of her skull. "Atticus is a good man, you know," she whispered. "Not quite like his father, but still ruthless in his own right. You know what makes him different?"

I shook my head as she typed in a code on the panel. "He feels things deep. He commits. When he loves, there's no going back. No matter what you do—what you ask of him. You'll get through this, Christine. I know it."

This woman was delusional. I was literally holding a

gun to her head and escaping their tower. I had a pile of bodies in my wake.

When the doors opened, I slid past her and stepped onto the elevator.

"Be safe, Christine. Have grace for my Atticus when he finds you. I know he'll have grace for you."

The doors shut and I breathed a sigh of relief. Despite the pain in my chest and the uncertainties surrounding my escape, I was proud of myself. I'd found my backbone and begun to see the world for what it was: a wild and unkind place, but also one where I could carve out a life for myself if I was strong enough. My body was tired from running and fighting, but my mind was sharper than it had ever been.

I'd escaped.

I'd gone from surviving to surviving with a purpose. The elevator doors opened and I stepped out, immediately finding myself in a small atrium with glass walls. The elevator doors closed behind me as I saw an opening to a large lush garden. The sun was bright and the plants were full of color. I could see a fountain at the center of it all and an iron gate that led to the outside world. I felt a rush of fresh air hit my face, and my heart pounded with a surge of adrenaline. Freedom. I was free and out from behind these walls. I could run away and take my chances. A smile crossed my face, and for a moment, I was free and light.

Then the realization hit me: I didn't want to run away. I wanted to be with Atticus, behind the walls of the DuPont estate, in the security of his arms. The idea sent a pang through my heart. It was a warm feeling, a familiar one.

But I couldn't be with him like this—with him owning me, his father toying with me, and resentment building a wall between us.

I had to leave. And I'd find all my men on my terms.

Or I'd die trying.

Chapter Thirteen

CHRISTINE

My childhood home was falling apart. No one had bothered to maintain it these years, and it broke my heart to see it so run down. The concrete stairs leading up to the front steps were cracked and weathered, the paint peeling on the trim. The grass was as tall as my waist and was dying from the fall weather. I could see my mother's garden that I'd always admired as a child, but its beauty was lost behind the vines.

The vines had overrun the house, their crimson leaves and deep purple blooms pushing up past the windowsills and clinging to the screens to block the view inside. The flowers were clinging to life but would be dead soon. Another few brisk morning chills, and the petals would fall. The leaves would turn brown and fall to the ground.

I could see the marble statuary of the fountain in the front, and the ivy had wrapped itself around the stone wolf I remembered from my childhood. The vines had grown even taller than the fountain, and I couldn't see beyond them. My mother's garden over-whelmed the gray brick with wild abandon, granting her a sense of freedom even in death. She'd always loved these beautiful flowers and had tended to them with such care and compassion. I wished she could see how beautifully they'd grown. My mother loved untamed things; maybe it's why I struggled so much with feeling controlled.

I pulled my hood tighter over my head and clutched it close. The leaves crunched under my boots as I made my way to the back door and slid my skeleton key into the lock. To my surprise, the door opened, revealing a time capsule of my childhood.

The wooden floors creaked with every step, and I dragged my hand along the old yellow wallpaper my father hated. Sheets covered the furniture in the sitting room. The sunlight came in through the windows, but the light was muted by the blood-red leaves and purple flowers clinging to the screens, blocking out the sun and casting a deep gloom over the room.

The air was unfamiliar, like the onset of winter—cold and dank.

The kitchen was overrun with cobwebs, and the counters were covered in dead flies. The leaves had invaded there too. The vines were on the countertops, crawling toward the cabinets and the ceiling. The molding was gunked up with paint, and the once-goddess room showed its age. Most of the paint had peeled off of the walls and showed the wooden slats. The room was dark, with a dark wood floor and dark brown walls. The curtains were thin and tattered, hanging haphazardly around the window.

It all looked so depressing and run-down.

I pulled out the burner phone I'd bought with money I'd stolen. The weight of it felt heavy in my palm, but I knew what I needed to do.

I dialed a phone number I memorized during my days of waiting for Atticus to return, the numbers a drone in my mind. A cold voice answered on the third ring.

"Hello?"

"Hello, Leo," I said while sitting down at the kitchen table and running the tips of my finger in the dust collected there. My tongue felt heavy and dry. I licked my lips and tasted dust. My anxiety was growing. I felt like I was suffocating, like the walls were closing in on me.

"Christine? Where are you? Are you safe?"

Muffled voices could be heard on the other end of the line. I had a feeling he'd be with Atticus and August.

"I'm safe. Probably the safest I've been in a while," I mused. A mouse crawled across the floor, scurrying away at the sound of my voice.

"Tell me where you are," he demanded.

"You'll find me," I whispered.

He let out a lingering sigh full of pain. "Christine, if this is about…"

"About our kiss? I thought you said we should forget it ever happened." A cold shiver ran down my spine. I tried to swallow, but my throat had turned to sandpaper.

He exhaled into the phone, and I pictured him running his hand through his long hair. "I'm sorry. Please, just tell me where you are."

I stroked my chin. "I'm not sure I can trust you with that just yet."

"I won't let anyone hurt you, or, or control you," he promised. "I'll give you whatever you want. We just want you to be safe, Christine."

"I'm not afraid of them hurting me, Leo. I'm afraid

of them controlling me." I sighed and leaned forward, my elbows resting on the table. "I can't change the past, but I can try to prevent the future." Lord Geralt had tried to own me. August had tried to possess my heart. Atticus wanted to control my every move.

"I know," he said, his voice strained. "I know. We'll let you be free. I promise."

"You won't *let* me do anything. I'm giving myself permission for once." I smiled softly, despite the tears streaming down my face. "I wanted to tell you, it was real for me, Leo. It wasn't a game or some trick. I really loved you."

"Loved?" I could hear movement and angry voices.

"Let me talk to her, Leo. You owe me that much. I need to hear her voice." August's tone was like a knife to the heart. I ached for him but wasn't ready to talk just yet.

"I have to go," I said.

"No," he pleaded. "Not yet. What will it take? Just tell me where you are. I can come alone or—or Augustus can come. Just tell me what you want and we'll make it happen. We're all so fucking worried about you. Atticus is…he's acting so strange."

I stayed silent as he argued with someone else in the room. The urge to hang up was strong, but I didn't want to end our conversation just yet.

"Christine?" I could hear his heavy breathing, the

sound of his fist pounding against the table. "I'm sorry. I'm sorry all of this happened the way it did. Give me a chance to make things right."

I chewed the inside of my lip. "Find me, Leo. I know you will, and when you get here, be prepared to follow my lead. You said once that you were on my side. It's time to prove it."

When I hung up the phone, thunder rumbled in the distance.

I was jolted awake by a sudden movement next to me. Disoriented, my eyes couldn't focus. The room was dark, and it took me a few moments to realize where I was.

The storm must have passed during the night, and the sun shone through the rotting curtains of the large window. The guest room was spacious, the windows were cracked, but sunlight still filtered in. A breeze flowed through the room, the humid air turning cool.

My arms and legs felt heavy, and my head ached. I rolled to my side to take in the sight of the beautiful wicker furniture and the stone fireplace. Memories of the last time I was here came flooding back, and I had to force myself not to cry.

"Dead," one of the maids whispered. "Both of them. The queen is coming to collect the child."

"I'm insulted that you thought it would be Leo to find you," Atticus's voice rumbled from the doorway.

My eyes flickered to where he stood. He had circles under his eyes and a desperate posture, his shoulders slumped as he drank in the sight of me. Atticus looked like something from my dream, like a scene from a gothic painting. Darkness, shadows, and light in equal parts. He was wearing a long black wool coat, the collar up and the top buttons undone.

"Are you here to take me back?"

His eyes brimmed with heat. Atticus stood dark and tall, looking at me with tired eyes. His hair was disheveled, his clothes wrinkled and damp. His hands were in fists, leaning against the doorjamb. He was breathing hard and fast, like he'd been running. "No," he whispered. "I'm here to fuck you so hard you can never run away from me again."

A switch flipped in me and I sat up, pushing the sheets off of my body. I was naked and exposed, but I didn't shy away, I didn't cover myself. I wanted him to see me, wanted him to look at me enough to realize that he couldn't control me.

"You think sex will fix this?" I asked.

"I think I damn well want to try."

I should have been afraid but I wasn't. I wasn't afraid of anything. I had been broken, shattered, and stitched back together, and I felt stronger, wiser, and more in control of my life.

"I lost you," he said after a long moment.

I smiled. "You didn't."

"Where have you been?" he demanded, his voice rough.

I tried to stand, but my legs felt weak. "Where is Leo?" I asked, my voice shaking.

Atticus stepped closer and closer until his chest was towering over me. He brushed my hair out of my eyes, and I met his gaze. "Don't ask me about other men when I'm standing here in front of you, looking at you." The scent of the outdoors clung to his skin and clothes, like he had been out in the rain the whole night.

"How did you know I was here?"

"I always know where you are, Little Monster. I could find you anywhere. Tell me why you left."

I swallowed the ball of emotion brewing in my throat. "You locked me up. Lied to August. And your father—"

"What about my father?"

My eyes shimmered with emotion. "He's not a good man, Atticus."

He looked solemnly at me. "Neither am I."

I reached out, my hand trembling as I touched him. His hand caught mine, and he pressed my palm against his cheek. "Yes, you are," I whispered. "Because I know you will change for me. I know you'll do whatever in your power to keep me safe but still give me autonomy over my own life."

He closed his eyes, and a single tear rolled down his cheek. "I thought I'd lost you. I thought…Christine," he whispered.

My heart burst at the sound of his voice, the concern in his tone. "I'm right here," I said and stood, pressing my chest against him.

He exhaled, and a slight smile crept across his face. "You killed twelve of my men, Little Monster," he whispered.

"They were in my way."

"I saw the footage of you fighting. You were ruthless. Breathing hard. Dragging a stolen blade across your enemy's throat without flinching."

"And yet you doubt me," I replied. I could feel his hard length pressing against my stomach.

"I don't doubt you. It's the rest of the world that I don't trust." His lips found mine, and he kissed me with the desperation of a man lost at sea. "I've missed you," he whispered.

"You left me for days, Atticus. You kept me in the

dark. I had no idea what was going on or where you were."

"If I had my way, you'd never leave my side."

"So stop pushing me away," I replied, my tone full of brimstone.

He grabbed my hips, digging into my flesh with his calloused hands. "I left the tower, still thinking how sweet your pussy tasted. Dreaming about how good you clenched my finger while you rode my palm." My breath hitched as he continued. "I wanted to fuck you, Little Monster. Make you scream my name. Claim you like a man claims the woman he loves. The woman he's watched and protected for years. The woman he'd do *anything* for."

I looked up at him. "So fucking claim me, Atticus."

My hands dropped to his belt, and I fumbled with the buckle for a moment before I pulled the belt free of his pants. He smirked, his eyes sparkling with lust as I slipped my fingers over the zipper. "I'm going to punish you for running away," he whispered.

"I'm counting on it," I replied, my lips curling into an answering smirk. I pushed the pants over his hips, and he kicked them aside. Nothing was going to keep us apart anymore. I wanted Atticus. Now. In this musty bedroom. With my hair a tangled mess. With the pain filling both our chests.

I wrapped my hand around his cock, brushing my thumb over the tip and collecting the few drops of moisture there. His breath caught, and he ground his hips against me. He reached into my hair, grabbing a fistful of strands and tugging hard enough to coax a moan from my lips. "Tell me how much you want my cock," he groaned.

I closed my eyes and leaned my forehead against his chest. His cock was hard, eager to be inside of me, and I wanted a break from the harsh realities of the world. I wanted to revel in the feeling of being wanted by this strong, towering, powerful man.

"Please," I murmured. "I need you inside of me."

His smile was wicked and dark. "On your knees, Little Monster." He took a step back and waited for me to kneel. I dropped to the floor and looked at his cock. Hard and thick, circumcised and veiny, the base covered in a messy trail of hair. I imagined how it would feel to have him pry my teeth apart and shove it into my mouth.

I leaned forward and ran my tongue over the head of his cock before gripping it with my trembling fingers, feeling his shaft pulse in my hand. I couldn't take him all in—not yet—but I kept my head tilted, flicking my tongue over the tip of his cock and spinning my tongue around the head.

"You tease," Atticus moaned, as he fisted his hands in my hair.

I slid my mouth down his shaft, taking him as deep as I could handle, and I rolled my tongue around the base of his cock. I reached between his legs, brushing my fingers over his balls as I slid my mouth back up. I looked up at him, my lips stretched wide over his shaft.

"I could live in your mouth, Little Monster," he muttered. "I want you to think of me with every word you speak."

I pulled my mouth off of him.

He smiled and reached down, yanking me to my feet. He then grabbed my thighs and lifted me up. I wrapped my legs around his waist, and he buried his face in my neck, his lips resting against my skin. I felt every muscle in his body tense as he carried me to the bed, but he didn't release me. He climbed on, slamming me down into the sheets, his lips finding mine.

His brown eyes looked down at me, half shut, heavy with lust. I reveled in his ravenous gaze, his full lips parted, his luscious hair tousled.

The bedsprings squeaked beneath us. He tore off his shirt, and his fingers circled my throat, his grip tight and unforgiving.

"Don't ever leave me again," he growled.

I kissed him, my tongue pushing through his lips,

mingling with his. He tasted like a thick, intoxicating cocktail of lust and power. His hands roamed my body and stroked my shoulders, my hips.

With his lips still pressed against mine, his hard body against mine, I reached down and grabbed his cock. I fisted it in my hand, stroking it hard and fast, feeling it pulse and grow even bigger beneath my palm.

"I'm going to fuck you, Little Monster."

He kissed me again then, shoving his tongue between my lips and peppering the corners of my mouth with his kiss. He rested his forehead against mine, his hips rolling against my hand, his cock swelling in my grip.

He pulled back, my hand falling from his cock.

"I love you," he whispered. The breathlessness of his voice made me weak. I wanted to feel every inch of him on my skin. I wanted to explore every bit of his dark soul.

He tilted my head to the side, exposing my neck.

Then he bit me.

I groaned, and he wrapped his hand around my throat, squeezing. "You're mine," he whispered.

My eyes widened and my body ached. I could feel his cock press against me, hard and heated, and I wanted him inside of me more than I wanted to breathe.

"I'm yours," I whispered.

He kissed me then. Aggressively. Intensely. Feeling. The weight of his body on mine.

His thumb moved to my jawline, his grip softening slightly. I cried out, my body erupting with heat when his cock slipped into me. He was desperate for me, his voice hoarse as he fucked me hard. He licked his tongue over my jaw and thrust in and out. It wasn't a slow, easy fuck. It was passionate. Claiming. It was damning and ruthless.

I was completely owned by him. There was no denying that. I was his and he was mine. The connection between us was thick and lustful. I clawed at his back, dug my nails in, and he howled, his voice deep and sultry. "Mine," he growled, gripping my throat and pinning me to the bed. I couldn't breathe, but I didn't need to. I was fine like that. Better, even.

"Yes," I managed to whine. "Yours."

He captured my lips, desperate.

"Christine…"

I was drowning in him, drowning in his voice, drowning in his touch. He ran his hands down my body, cupped my breasts and squeezed. "Atticus!" I cried and pushed up against him. He was fucking me hard and I was close. He was beyond filthy; he was rough and demanding. It was hard, forceful. I could barely breathe, and he was completely filling me. His cock was throbbing, growing impossibly harder. I begged for him to make me feel good, begged for him to keep going, begged for him to fuck me harder and harder. He thrust in and out of me, fast and merciless.

He shifted, and the angle of his cock hit deeper within me.

"Oh God," I whimpered, my body arching up off the bed. "Please! Atticus!" I was desperate for him, desperate for him to fill me, desperate to satisfy this need for him. He slowed down, ran his hands through my hair and kissed me again.

There was no way to fight against this. There was no way to deny it. This was what I wanted. I wanted this connection. I wanted to be his and I wanted to be his Little Monster. I wanted him to own me, hurt me, love me, and fuck me.

He pulled my knees over his shoulders and wrapped his arm around my waist, lifting me slightly off the bed. The new position drove him deeper into me. "Atticus!" I cried. His breath was harsh against my lips as our kiss was more demanding. His teeth brushed against my lower lip, my body shaking as his cock stroked my G-spot.

"I love the sounds you make. Keep screaming my name, Little Monster. Keep begging. I've dreamed of this for years." The pleasure in his tone was raw and savage. It was hot, the friction delicious, the pressure amazing. The way he looked at me made me melt.

"Please," I begged, my voice breathless, my body aching for more. He captured my lips, kissing me roughly.

"So close," he whispered.

I was on the edge, and he knew. The way his voice changed, the way he looked at me, the way he fucked me. I wanted more of him. I wanted him to touch me, to grab my hair and do unspeakable things to me.

Then all of a sudden, he pulled out of me and yanked me up before spinning me around and shoving me facedown onto the bed. My hair was pushed into my face, and I could barely see. An empty feeling settled over me. I immediately hated the loss of him, and a sad whimper escaped my lips. "Never fucking leave me again," he snapped. "If you leave, I will find you." He slapped my ass, sending a searing pain to travel through my senses. "If you run, I'll catch you." He slapped me again, this time harder. "And if you try to hide? Oh, Little Monster, I'll check under the bed and pull you out by your neck."

His words should have frightened me. It was an intensity—an obsession—that would make any normal girl run.

But I was thrilled. I was so incredibly turned on that I could barely breathe.

"Atticus, I need you again," I pleaded.

"You feel that? How empty your pretty little cunt feels? How much you ache for me to continue? That's how I feel every goddamn day of my life. I'm going to fuck you so deep and so hard…" he growled, before I felt his cock press against my entrance. "You'll finally understand why there's no way in hell you'll ever get rid of me."

I clenched my teeth together, my body stiff, as he filled me up again. He grabbed my hair and yanked it back, my breasts exposed.

I screamed into the comforter, my body writhing under his. I was completely overwhelmed by the intensity of his words and the force with which he made love to me. He continued to fuck me with his cock and his fingers, his hand moving to my ass, squeezing hard.

The pain was exquisite. The fire burned in my belly, my heart beating wildly.

"Take me from behind, Little Monster," he murmured. "I want to see your back. I want to feel your skin on my hands, on my lips. I want to feel your heart pounding."

He moved faster, his hips slamming up. My body was shaking from the pleasure and the desire. "Come for me, Little Monster," he coaxed. "Come for me, now." He slammed into me again, and I felt the pressure build. He pounded into me, and his roughness drove me over the edge. My body quivered and shook. I was screaming, screaming Atticus's name and clawing the bedsheets. He released my hair, and I collapsed on top of the bed, but he gripped my hips and pulled me back into him, still thrusting. I felt my body shake with pleasure. I felt the wetness pool between my legs.

He groaned, his body tensing as the pleasure washed over him. He was shaking, shuddering. He held my wrists, his cock throbbing inside of me as he came.

I felt his seed fill my body, and I felt warm, safe, and protected. He kissed me, releasing my wrists and petting my body gently. "I love you, Little Monster. Don't ever fucking leave me again."

"I love you, too," I replied, my body still trembling. "Don't try to control me again."

"It's not that easy," he replied. "I can't lose you."

"You won't...I promise." I kissed his cheek. "But you will lose me if you treat me like property. I can't do that. I didn't escape Lord Geralt three years ago to be owned by another. I refuse."

He went still. "You think I'm like Lord Geralt?"

My heart thudded. I didn't want to ruin our moment, but he needed to understand. Propping myself up, I looked deeply into his eyes. "No. You're not. But I didn't fight hard to overcome everything just to sit back and let you take the reins. I've earned the right to stand at your side, Atticus."

He tucked my blonde hair behind my ear. "Okay," he replied.

"Really?"

He sighed. "I can't promise that I won't go to great lengths to protect you. I've built my entire life around you, Christine. Followed you. Made your life easier. Observed you from a distance. It's not…easy for me to give that up. But I refuse to make you feel trapped."

"What if I want to be trapped?" I teased, kissing his heated lips. He laid us gently down on the bed, pulling the sheets over us. "Trapped under your body. Trapped on your co—"

"You're going to be the death of me," he moaned.

I kissed his cheek. "Not a chance in hell, Atticus."

Chapter Fourteen

"Augustus and Leo are on their way here," Atticus said while stroking my arm. He spoke in a detached, pained voice full of regret. He had a faint odor of sandalwood and musk, a clean scent that made me want to bury my nose in his neck.

"You told August I was alive?" I asked.

"Leo did. When you left, we were worried sick."

I chewed on my lip. "How did he react?"

Atticus narrowed his eyes at me. "How do you think?"

"I think he would have been overjoyed." I swallowed hard to keep the emotion back.

"That you were alive? Absolutely. That I lied? He was livid. The fact that you left made him practically feral. I've never seen him so determined, so…" His voice was deep and tinged with turmoil.

"King-like?" I finished for him. "Would you have told him if I hadn't left?"

Atticus sat up. "No. My plan was to keep you hidden until Lord Nathan was dealt with. We had no choice. You left. You didn't come to us. We had to find you." Atticus's voice caught. "We had to know if you were okay."

"I'm sorry. I thought it was best that I left. I didn't get a chance before, but Atticus, I think you need to know a few things about your father. He…he threatened me. Called me a whore. Said you were just using me for more power. Is…is that true?" At my question, the tension in the room climbed. The air practically felt thick and heavy, almost like stepping into the sauna.

"The fact that you're even asking me that is further proof that I've been a grave disappointment to you. Of course not, Christine. I became powerful so that I could protect you. Take care of you. I beat my way to the top of my father's empire with one goal in mind—you. I don't care if you're queen. I don't care about titles or money. I just…" He squeezed me tighter. "My father will pay for this."

I nuzzled his neck, too emotional to speak. "I don't think we can trust him, Atticus. And your mother…"

My voice trailed off. It was hard to imagine such a fragile, submissive woman raising such a powerful man like Atticus.

A booming sound came from downstairs, the front door slamming open and thudding against the wall. "Christine!" August screamed. I sat up in bed as his boots pounded up the creaky stairs. "Christine!"

I quickly got out of the bed Atticus and I shared and wrapped the sheet around me, not wanting August to find us like this.

"Here we go," Atticus said with a curse.

August threw open the door, his face flaming red. "You're here. You're really here." August's voice cracked.

I stared at him, unsure what to say.

August crossed the room and strode over to me, grabbing me by the arms. "Christine, I'm sorry. I'm so sorry." He cried, kissing me all over my face. "I love you so much. I was so scared."

I squeezed his hand and nodded, too distraught to speak.

"I thought I'd never see you again." The agony in his words seared my heart as he clung to me, breathing me in. His despair felt like a thousand needles plunging into my skin.

"August!" I exclaimed, tears streaming down my cheeks. His sharp intake of breath sent chills down my spine, and I could feel his warm tears on my skin. His hands, still shaking, reached out to grasp my upper arms as if he didn't believe I was real.

Our faces were but inches apart and time stood still. His brown eyes and my own blue ones locked in an intense gaze, a myriad of emotions and memories passing between us. His lips lingered by mine for just a moment before he pulled away, trembling and over-whelmed.

Behind me, the air seemed to thicken with tension as Atticus watched our reunion from the shadows. His presence seemed to sap all the heat from the room as I tried to rationalize what this meant for us all.

August's voice was barely a whisper. "Say my name again…please, Christine."

My heart fluttered in my chest as I uttered that sweet name once more. "August…"

We stared at each other for what felt like an eternity before August turned to Atticus. His expression was a mix of anger and confusion, his jaw clenched. He looked from me to Atticus, back to me again. "Tell me, Christine. Were you in on the lies, too?"

I shook my head. "No. Atticus took me to the tower. I fought him and…"

"Why didn't you call me when you escaped?" he asked.

I bit my lip. "I needed a moment to…process everything."

August nodded. "And you processed it with the man who lied to me?"

An angry growl came from Atticus's throat. "That's enough," Atticus said in a hoarse voice.

August let go of me, but he never took his eyes off of me. "I wish I could say I'm surprised you waited hours to call me, Atticus, but it seems on trend for you to keep secrets. It's time for you to leave."

Atticus stood and crossed his arms. Thankfully, he'd put on his pants before August had gotten here. "I'm not going anywhere." He was muscular and barrel-chested, with a face as harsh as rusted metal.

August shook his head. "You've done enough!" he roared. "You're the reason she ran away. You lied to me, Atticus. You fucking lied. Held me while I sobbed for her. Yelled at me when I was grieving."

My stomach clenched. The air crackled with tension as August and Atticus sized each other up.

Atticus took a menacing step forward. "I made you man up so you could do what you needed to do. Christine was never going to be safe at that castle, and you know it."

One of August's eyes twitched. "I could have kept her safe." The air between Atticus and August was heavy with rage and mistrust.

"You didn't keep her safe three years ago!" Atticus spat venomously. "You didn't protect her when she was weak and broken in Harvington. And you didn't guard her at that engagement party. I did. I've been the one who has always been there for her. So sorry I didn't trust a reckless prince to take responsibility for the woman I love."

A suffocating tension filled the room. My heart burned intensely, like a fire blazing out of control and searing my veins with every beat.

"It's true," August hissed. His voice was strained and defeated. "You did keep her safe. And you're right. I never could have done that."

"August, don't," I pleaded. "It wasn't your fault—"

He threaded his fingers through mine. "I'm sorry, Christine. I will spend the rest of my life giving you everything you deserve. I will be a good husband to you. A good king to my people."

I nodded. "I know." I'd always seen the potential in August. I knew that his ability to love fiercely was his strongest attribute.

He turned to Atticus. "I owe Christine a million apologies, and I will make this right. However, I'm not apologizing to you. Not now. Maybe not ever. You lied to me. You fucking lied to me and you watched me break down, Atticus. You held me as I cried."

I gasped, shocked by the picture August was painting. I could taste bile in the back of my throat and the metallic bite of blood where my teeth had sunk into my bottom lip. I didn't want them to fight like this, but I knew it was necessary—knew we needed to air all of this out so we could move forward.

A cloud passed over Atticus's face, and he parted his lips to argue, but he stopped. "You're right."

August nodded. "I'm going to make Christine happy." He stroked my cheek. "I love you, Christine." He then turned to Atticus. "But you, you deserve to be punished for what you did. For lying to the king."

Atticus's face was expressionless. "I deserve it, but I won't feel sorry for protecting Christine when you couldn't."

August's voice boomed like thunder, shaking the air around us. "Says the man that locked her up," he spat, glaring at me. Then he turned back with determination. "I'm going to take you to the castle. I'm going to take care of you—"

"NO!" I yelled, refusing him before he could finish.

My feet were perched on a precipice of rock, surrounded by two roaring men who loved me in different ways, and I felt like I was plummeting into cold darkness.

"What do you mean?"

"I won't go to the castle!"

August's face fell. "You don't want to be with me?"

I stroked his cheek tenderly. "Of course I want to be with you."

My answer made Atticus gasp with pain and clutch his chest. I reached out to Atticus, but August caught my hand before I could make contact. I ended up reaching in the middle, and my fingers brushed against Atticus's collarbone before August took my hand to his lips and kissed the back of my fingers.

I shook my head with dainty refusal. "I want to be with *both* of you——"

August deflated and took a step back. "Absolutely not. Atticus can't be trusted," he replied forcefully.

Atticus remained silent. Rolling my shoulders back, I looked August in the eye. "I'm not going back to that castle, August. Not now, at least. Atticus is right. We are in danger and we need to take down Lord Nathan." I paused to look at Atticus. "But we're going to do it together."

"I'm not working with him," August sneered.

"You don't have a choice, August." I tipped my chin up and stared at him. "Because I'm with Atticus. I'm with you. And if I'm being honest, I'm with Leo, too. I ran away because I want all of us to work together. I want all of us to be safe."

August shook his head. "I can't believe you're asking this of me. After everything he's done. You have no idea what it was like, Christine. I've never been so…"

When his words trailed off, he clutched me closer, as if he wanted to feel that I was really here—really alive.

August looked at me with a pleading expression. "If you don't want to go to the castle, then fine. Let me take you somewhere else, Christine. Anywhere. We can even stay in this—" He looked around at the dismal state of my childhood home. "Here. Just you and me against the world, love. We can—"

"No." I shook my head. "It's all of us or nothing, August." His face was conflicted, so I stroked his cheek. "I'm tired of being hurt and kept apart from the people I love."

August frowned, and his grip loosened. "I don't want you to hurt."

I shook my head. "I'm not going to run away from my feelings anymore."

"Christine, I can't trust him. I can't…share. You've been mine since the day I met you. I've loved you, adored you for as long as I can remember." He looked at Atticus with disgust. "Am I not enough?"

"August," I said, yanking his attention back to me. "Do you love me?"

His face softened. "More than life."

"Then you will love me as I am. You will work together. For us."

He looked at Atticus with a fierce glare. "I still don't trust him. You lied to me, locked her up, and belittled me every fucking step of the way. You're a criminal. A monster."

"I know I'm a monster," Atticus growled. He stalked toward us, standing just a breath away from August. "But I'm *her* monster. She loves me, even though she shouldn't. Even though I probably don't deserve it. So I'll work with you, King Augustus, whether you like it or not." He lowered his voice. "You got a small taste of what it's like to be without her. I suggest you do everything in your power to never feel that way again."

Without another word, Atticus left the room. There was a deafening silence between August and me. After I heard the front door close, I turned to August.

"I know this is hard," I whispered.

"I don't like him, Christine. I don't like any of this." I sighed and placed my forehead against his chest.

"I know," I whispered. "But I stopped letting the

rest of the world make decisions for me three years ago. It's all or nothing, August."

And I leaned into him, trusting him to hold me up.

He brushed a hair out of my face and traced the crest of my cheekbone with his thumb. "Alright. All of us against the fucking world."

I nodded. "All of us."

Chapter Fifteen

August's face glared across the table with a vicious grimace. His lips were curled into a snarl, and his eyes shot daggers of hate. At the other end in a worn chair, Atticus sat with his arms crossed over his chest, glaring right back. In between them was the remains of fast-food takeout. Dirty plates, paper cups and cutlery cluttered the surface. I sat right in the middle with my fist under my chin, waiting for someone to say something.

"Leo should be here soon," Atticus grumbled.

"Oh, does my guard report to you, now?" August asked. His eyes had narrowed to slits and his lips were pulled back to expose his teeth. "It's not enough that the two of you were scheming together, but now you're best friends, too?"

"Maybe he has more faith in my leadership abilities," Atticus said flatly. "And do I detect a hint of jealousy? I didn't realize you cared so deeply for our friendship."

I dug my fingernails into the tabletop in frustration. Getting the two of them to work together was much harder than I thought. The wood beneath my nails was rough from age and felt like splinters and sandpaper—just like their friendship.

"You can rot together in hell!" August yelled. He leaned back in his chair and scowled. "We're not friends. Never were."

"August," I whispered. "Please calm down." August had no idea just how much Atticus had done for him behind the scenes. It was a twisted situation I didn't know how to navigate. He needed to know the truth, but I wasn't sure if he was in the right headspace to hear it.

"I am calm," he sulked.

Loud raps on the front door rumbled through the room, followed by a pause, and then another series of sharp knocks. August and Atticus looked expectantly at me.

"I suppose I'll answer it then," I said before getting up. Nerves had my limbs shaking.

"You okay, Little Monster?" Atticus asked in a quiet voice.

"I'll be fine," I said with a weary smile. "I need to speak to him."

August and Atticus watched me closely, and I thought I saw the tiniest glimmer of solidarity and understanding pass between them, but then August spoke, ruining it all.

"When you're done chatting with Leo, tell him to see me so I can fire him."

"You cannot fire him, August," I said while pinching the bridge of my nose.

"Like hell I can't!"

"That's what Augustus does when he doesn't get his way. Just runs from the problem."

"Oh, like you would know, you son of a bitch!"

I left them to bicker and walked down the long hallway leading to the front door. With a shaky breath, I twisted the knob. The hinges groaned and Leo stood on my doorstep with a look of expectation.

Leo's breaths were deep and throaty, like his lungs were trying to drag air in by force. He was shaking, his hands fiddling with his silver rings and the leather of his vest. "Guess it was Atticus that found you," he said softly.

A breeze picked up his hair, making it float around him as he stared at me.

"Atticus *wanted* to find me," I said, pain lacing my words. "I'm not sure you did, considering the way we left things."

Leo frowned. "Of course I wanted to fucking find you," he said slowly. Leo took a step closer, grazing my arm with his as he invaded my space, his body radiating heat like a furnace. "You think I wasn't worried sick? You think I haven't been pacing the streets of Aldrich looking for you all night?"

"Leo," I said softly. I could feel a now familiar tingle race up my spine. Leo's presence was like a drug, his touch addicting. His presence triggered something primal inside me, a need for him that was hard to deny. A need for him to hold me, to tell me everything was going to be okay.

"Do you want a declaration?" he asked. "Is that it? You want to know how I can't fucking focus when you're in the room? Do you want to know how I have to force myself to tear my eyes away from your beautiful face? Should I tell you that my heart races when you're near? Should I get down on my knees and beg you to pick me? Stay with me? Will that convince you, Christine?" He grabbed my chin. "What will it take? Because the truth is, I was fucking terrified that something happened to you. I was scared that I was making the wrong choice in trusting Atticus. I agonized every single night you slept in that goddamn castle."

"I never meant to make you worry," I said.

I looked at Leo, love and pain swirling like a tornado in my gut. I observed the way his shirt stretched across his shoulders and the way his eyes were pained. How the morning light made him look like he was made of marble. I wanted to dig my fingers into the ridges of his stomach and hold onto him forever. I could feel drops of tears collect and well up, flooding my eyes until I couldn't see. I reached out to stroke his stubble-covered chin. "I'm sorry, I just—"

His lips took mine, and I didn't have time to say another word. Leo's tongue swirled around my own, probing and demanding. He grabbed my waist and pulled me against him. Leo spun us around and pinned me against the doorframe. My head thumped against the wood. The corner of the doorframe left bite marks on my skin, as Leo's hands bruised my hips, his lips so soft but demanding.

He kissed me, hard and urgent.

"Christine, I can't—" he whispered.

I cut off his words with another kiss. His skin

smelled sweet like soap and rain and the clean cotton of his shirt. My back arched as Leo's hands roamed over my body. His fingers trailed down my spine and squeezed my hips before wrapping around my ass. I gasped and Leo's tongue plunged into my mouth. I wrapped my arms around his neck, relishing in the heat radiating off his body.

"Oh great. Now she's kissing him," August said. Leo tore his mouth from mine, and we both snapped our attention to the hallway, where Atticus and August were standing with their arms crossed over their chest.

"I personally didn't think he had it in him," Atticus said, his eyes twinkling with something I didn't understand.

"Fuck off, Atticus," Leo said. He grabbed my hand, pulled me into the house, and slammed the door behind us. We were both still breathing hard. I fought the urge to feel embarrassed. This was what I wanted, right? All of them. Together.

"So, since we're all here. What the hell happened?" Leo asked, ever the practical one.

"I left DuPont tower," I said while tugging him toward the sitting room. Atticus and August followed after us. I took a moment to remove the sheets covering the furniture, then plopped down on my mother's favorite sofa, with Leo sitting beside me.

"Is it wrong that I'm a little happy she killed some of your men in the process?" August asked while preening at Atticus. He moved to the large wingback and slumped into it.

"I'm about two seconds from punching him," Atticus said while staring at me.

"Did you get hurt?" Leo asked, unbothered by their fighting. The golden guard looked at me closely, searching my eyes for the pain we both knew was there. Even though I could turn my emotions off during a kill, I still struggled with the aftermath. I refused to feel bad for escaping, though. Atticus might have had some sway, but Theodore DuPont was bad news. I had a bad feeling something terrible would happen if I stayed there any longer.

"I'm fine," I replied. "It needed to be done. We're all here now, and we're going to work together to take down Lord Nathan."

August let out an audible scoff.

"Augustus," Atticus said. He cleared his throat. "We know you might have some reservations, but we need you. I know it doesn't seem like it, but *everything* I've done has been in your best interest."

August narrowed his eyes and looked at us suspiciously. "My best interest? Stealing the woman I am to marry was *in my best interest?*"

I swallowed. "Atticus, maybe we should tell him."

"Tell me what?" August snapped.

Leo looked between us. Observing. *Always* observing. I squeezed his hand while Atticus gnawed nervously on his lip.

I gave a brief nod to the towering DuPont, who was stewing in his indecision. "Six weeks ago, your mother came to me. She had a job for me to do."

At the mention of his mother, August's face fell. I hadn't had a chance to talk to him about her death, and the loss of Isabelle still weighed heavily on both of us. "What kind of job?" he choked out.

"Your father got some information—information that put you in danger. Your father was very angry."

August peered at him. "Did you—"

"I killed your father to protect you," Atticus said, cutting him off.

August sat back on the seat, his eyes wide with wonder. "You? *You* killed him?" He leaned forward and gaped at Atticus. "What did he find out? What did he know?"

"Your mother had an affair. You are not the rightful heir to the throne," Atticus said. His declaration was like a heavy weight settling over all of us. It was a complete and naked truth. My fingers were clenched so tight around Leo's hand that the tips of my fingers hurt and tingled.

"You're lying," August said in disbelief. His breathing quickened as his fingers twitched in his lap. August's eyes darted from me to Atticus to Leo, looking for some sign of deception.

"I'm not," Atticus replied.

Silence stretched. Our breathing seemed too loud, even the creaks and groans of my childhood home were deafening, weaving through the silence that had fallen over us.

August's teeth ground together like gears. His fingers flexed like he was going to tear something apart. "You really are a fucking bastard," August finally said, his voice was barely above a whisper. "What is your angle? Why lie like this?" August stood from his seat and moved toward the fireplace, his boots thudding against the floor.

"Augustus," Atticus said. I could hear the crack in his voice. "Your father was going to kill you and your mother."

"No. My father was a bastard, but he wouldn't—" His eyes slid to me and he paled. He'd learned a lot about King Frederick these last couple of weeks and exactly what he was capable of.

Atticus stepped toward him. "I know you don't want

to believe me, but it's true. She made me promise to keep you safe—"

"Stop," August said. He held up his hands. "Stop. I don't want to hear this."

"August. I know this is hard," I said, trying not to anger him more.

August's eyes widened as he looked back at me. "Christine?" He paused as he took a deep breath. "You knew. Why didn't you tell me?" Anger seethed from him, his shoulders hunched and his cracked knuckles turned white.

"I-I was going to," I stuttered. "I just found out while I was at DuPont tower. I would have told you earlier, but we were..." My words trailed off. We were dealing with our fucked up relationship. We were trying to navigate all of this chaos.

"I wanted to tell you," Atticus added. "But you weren't stable. I wasn't sure—"

August's nostrils flared. "Don't you fucking dare," he said to him. "You are a fucking liar," he shrieked. "You lied about Christine and now you're lying about this. I don't know what you want, but I don't believe this shit. I don't believe a fucking word."

"It's true," Atticus said. "And I have proof."

August snorted. "More lies?

Atticus rummaged through his pocket and pulled out an envelope.

"What the hell is that?" August asked before taking it from him, giving us all a look of disbelief. He slowly opened it, and a piece of paper slid out.

August's fingers trembled as he unfolded the note, and he gripped the edges. He stared at the paper, his eyes skimming the words, then looked back up to us. His brown eyes spoke of incredulity.

"You know it's authentic. You've seen your mother's handwriting plenty of times," Atticus said.

August swiped at the tears welling up in his eyes. "Why do you have this?"

"Insurance," Atticus whispered. "When she told me to kill the king, I asked her to write down the truth and sign it. I've kept it safe, but wanted to have something should she stab me in the back."

August cleared his throat.

"Dear Augustus,

If you're reading this, then I'm hoping Atticus has a good reason for telling you the truth." Tears welled up in his eyes. *"I'm so sorry, my dearest boy, but I have not been honest with you..."*

He dropped the paper and crumpled to the floor. I got up from my seat and wrapped my arms around him as he sobbed. I stroked his hair as his tears soaked into my chest. His shoulders shook as he cried. Then, he went strangely still and tilted his head up to look at Atticus, fear brimming in his expression. "If King Frederick was not my father, then who is?"

Atticus DuPont looked up and his face was on full display. He was pale, bloodless and trembling before August. His brown eyes, once so bright and certain, were now clouded and despairing. "August, you're a DuPont."

Chapter Sixteen

ATTICUS

I'd let Augustus spend the day sulking in the study. He'd disappeared for two hours after I dropped the bomb in his lap that we were brothers, and when he returned, he clutched a bottle of cheap whiskey and was stomping through the house, looking for a private room to drink away his sorrows.

Christine stayed hidden in the bedroom, trying to avoid his anger and also trying to sort through her own feelings about everything. I was giving her space and *also* reluctantly giving Leo the chance to grow some balls and comfort her.

If he didn't pull the stick up his ass out soon and go

take care of our girl, *I* would. And every miserable bastard in this house would hear her scream my name.

I opened the door to the study and walked inside, prepared for the worst. Augustus was temperamental, selfish, and self-destructive even under the best conditions. It wouldn't surprise me if he was high off his ass and close to finishing the bottle.

What I found surprised me. Augustus was sitting behind the desk, just so, with his legs crossed, the bottle in his grasp, his eyes fixed on the bookshelf lining the opposite wall.

The study was warm. The setting sun danced and glittered through the panes, warming the rich oak and hardwood floors. A wall of books was on the right, and an expansive window was behind Augustus.

"I used to like reading."

I didn't say anything. He looked up at me after a moment, and I saw the glassy look in his eyes.

"Graphic novels. I liked the pictures. Too many words on a page and I got bored, but I liked it enough." He took a swig of his whiskey. "King Frederick told me to stop *wasting time with frivolous things.*" He swallowed. "So I stopped reading them."

He was speaking slowly, but with a clarity that I hadn't heard come from his mouth in years. Maybe ever.

"I also liked sailing," he said again, and then he reached for the bottle and pulled it back to his lips.

I stood next to him and looked at the books lined up in perfect order. There was a world atlas, but the spine was worn down, the pages well-thumbed.

"I used to read about the oceans," he said, "and dream about sailing around the world."

His voice slurred and his eyes were glossed over. He was a mess. And it was my fault. I spied another bottle of whiskey and took a swig while he spoke, needing my own liquid courage to survive the tension. The whiskey had a sharp, sweet taste that bit back, like a quaking cramp in my gut. Its smooth, woody taste was hard to describe but easy to enjoy.

"I wanted to just be gone for a long time. For as long as I could remember, I dreamed about escaping the responsibilities of the Crown. But I never imagined it would be possible. Now…now I hardly know who I am anymore."

I didn't know what to say.

"I guess it makes sense that we're related, doesn't it? Both of us never wanted the lives we were handed," he said before looking up at me again, but his eyes were unfocused. I opened my mouth to protest, but he waved his hand. "I saw you come home with bloody knuckles, your eyes wide like you'd seen a ghost. I never asked about it, mostly because I knew you'd never tell me. Also, because I didn't see the point."

"I wouldn't have told you," I admitted. It wasn't his burden to bear.

"Where's Christine?" he asked suddenly, and then he leaned forward, knocking into the desk and sending the whiskey bottle to the floor. I stepped in and caught it before spilling more than a few drops. He looked at me with a furious glare and then pushed his chair back. "Christine," he growled. "Where the fuck is she?"

"She's resting," I said, standing back.

"I need to call off the engagement," he said.

He fell forward and hit the floor hard. I hurried around the desk just as he started to roll, his arm flailing out, knocking books to the floor.

I reached out, fingers closing around his forearm, just above the elbow, and hauled him upright. "You will do no such thing."

He scrunched his face up and looked at me. "What's the point? Why fight Lord Nathan, Atticus? Yeah, he's a prick. But if he's telling everyone I'm not the rightful king, then it seems to me I just got out of running the kingdom. That's a *good* thing. Christine won't have to go back to that damn castle. I won't have to disappoint everyone. Win. Win. Win."

"That's some selfish shit. Don't you think?" I chastised him, shaking his arm. He frowned and then looked toward the bookshelf. "Let's get you to bed."

He bumped into me, pushing me back. I stumbled and then looked down to see him sitting on the floor. He was still staring at the damn bookshelf. I followed his gaze, and sure enough, his eyes were tracking the spine of one book, which was facing back toward the wall. He reached over, his fingers wrapping around it, and then he pulled it out.

"Look at that," he said in his raspy voice. "A photo album."

He wiped dust off the spine and pried it open with sluggish hands, staring at each photo like the images were precious. "Here's a photo at a diplomats' dinner," he said. "Christine looks so tiny."

I peered over his shoulder to look at the photo and smiled at the image. Christine was wearing a frilly pink dress and holding her mother's hand, a broad smile stretched across her face.

"And here's one of me," he continued. "It's the State Dinner for Oak Palace, I think. I was ten, maybe? So young. The House of Rose always accompanied us to all the functions."

"You look like a prick," I joked, nudging his side.

Christine's father stood beside him, and on the

other side was King Frederick, who looked as snide then as he did the day he died.

Augustus's fingers trailed over the photo, the warm fireplace, the fancy dress uniforms. He closed the album and then looked back up at me; his face was blank. "Frederick tried to teach me how to rule the country," he said, wiping at his eyes. "They tried to groom me and turn me into a king. But I never wanted it, and I'm not good enough to do it. I'm not a good man, Atticus. I am not a good king. I never wanted to be. This is my chance, you know?"

"Augustus, I think you need to—"

My voice was cut off by Leo barging into the room. His green eyes were wide with worry. "We have a problem."

Augustus tried to stand but was too drunk. Fuck. "What's going on?"

Leo ran his hands through his hair. "Lord Nathan attacked two Houses today. The House of Pearl and the House of Brooke."

I scrunched my face up in confusion. "What purpose does he have for doing this?"

Leo shook his head. "At first, I wasn't sure. They're high-ranking Houses but still a strange target." He eyed something on the bookshelf and snapped his fingers. "But then I got to thinking," he said before marching over to a collection of scrolls and flipping through them.

"Can you think a little quieter? My head hurts," Augustus complained, testing my patience.

When Leo found the scroll he was looking for, he yanked it out and unrolled it on the desk. I peered at it. "This is the bloodline for the throne. What does this have to do with anything?"

He dragged his finger along the parchment and pointed at the bottom. "Here is Lord Nathan. House of Redwood. Unimpressive. Lower ranking. About eight hundred people have to die before he gets into power."

I shrugged. Lord Nathan would have to spill a lot of blood before he was even close, and even though he was gaining momentum, he didn't have the resources for an all-out war. "But here," Leo added. "Here are the Houses attacked today. No survivors."

Augustus pulled himself up and leaned on the desk to look at what Leo was saying.

"King Frederick had no brothers. His cousin was disqualified when he was imprisoned twelve years ago. Augustus was his only son. Since there is no family, by law, the Crown defers to the highest ranking house in the kingdom. Lord Galvin Hunt, House of Pearl, was next in line after Augustus. Dead," Leo said.

"I never liked him," Augustus slurred.

"Lord Melvin Hunt, Lady Hattie Hunt, then Lord Vasille Greene. All dead." In one simple, coordinated attack, Lord Nathan had wiped out the next four in line for the throne.

Leo let out a shaky sigh. "And then fifth in line," he said, the pad of his finger landing on a familiar photo.

"No," Augustus breezed, sobriety coming to him like a painful slap.

Leo looked up at us. "The House of Rose."

I snapped my attention up. "No. Everyone thinks Christine is dead. They won't defer to her." Bile licked my tongue, and saliva puddled in the back of my mouth as fear of the unknown came to the fore.

Leo didn't seem convinced. "Christine just made a big show of escaping DuPont tower. I easily found out what you were up to, and who knows how many informants Lord Nathan has? What if...what if he plans to prove Augustus isn't the rightful heir? What if he uses the contract King Frederick signed to their family to marry off Christine? The lords will honor it out of fear."

"Making him...the next king," Augustus said, his tone deadly. The words left his lips, emblazoned in white fire, burning through the heavy tension in the room.

"No," I argued. "We have to continue as if Christine is dead. It's the only way."

"And what if Lord Nathan continues to kill to get his way?" Christine asked. We all spun around to face the door. She stood there with her shoulders rolled back, the silk of her robe falling delicately off her shoulder. She chewed on her top lip for a moment while observing us.

"Let him paint the streets red," I said. "Kill them all. I'm not letting him get close to you. The best course of action is to continue to let the world think you're dead."

She shook her head. "The best course of action is for me to marry August immediately. Like, right now. If I'm next in line, then this solves everything."

Leo shook his head. "I don't like this."

I stroked my chin. "It's actually brilliant. If the two of you marry now, it secures Augustus's spot as king and protects Christine. All we need is a wedding ceremony."

We all looked to Augustus, who was still drunk, still a broken mess. "Christine, I'm not sure I *want* my place secured."

Fuck it all. I boomed with anger. "You don't get the luxury of backing out, Augustus. The alternative is Lord Nathan marrying her."

Christine's eyes sparkled with sadness. "Do you not want to marry me, August?"

He straightened and marched over to her, cupping her cheek in his palm. "Of course I want to marry you. I've never wanted anything more. It's just…a lot right now."

Christine ran her hands across Augustus's chest with frailness and fear. She touched his face with softness, a tender caress from his chin to his lips. "I know, but the plan was always for us to get married, right?"

Augustus looked at Leo and me. We hadn't even begun to navigate our tumultuous relationship but didn't have the luxury of time. "Of course, love. I want you. I *adore* you. I'm just a little fucked in the head right now. And then it's not just me. I'm still coming to terms with the idea of knowing two other men possess your heart, too."

His forehead creased and her bottom lip quivered. I took a step closer to the two of them and put my hand on Christine's back. "A lot has happened and we still have a lot to figure out," I said quietly. "But we need to move quickly. Lord Nathan will know that his attack has revealed his plan. We don't have much time."

Augustus let out a deep sigh. "When?"

Christine turned to look at him. "I suppose you should sober up. We need to find a church. Have formal witnesses. The certificate. We also need to announce that I'm *alive*."

"The lords won't recognize a wedding unless we follow the proper protocols. They'll need to be in attendance," Augustus said.

Leo's mouth hit the floor. "Don't you think this is all a little sudden?"

"Maybe," Christine replied with a smile. "But I don't want to marry Lord Nathan, and I absolutely want to protect all of you. This will solidify our position."

Augustus stared at Christine, processing the simple way in which she spoke. None of this was romantic or thoughtful, and I wondered if it bothered my brother to have such a clinical approach to supposedly the happiest day of his life.

I personally was trying not to think of it too much. I knew that eventually Christine would marry Augustus. I'd resigned myself to that future of living on the sidelines, accepting scraps of her affections like a greedy addict. But now the reality of it all was staring us both right in the face.

Augustus spoke to Christine. "Are you sure?"

"Yes," she said quickly, the word coming out in a fast exhale of air.

"Absolutely sure?"

She hesitated. "Absolutely."

Augustus cleared his throat. "Alright." His voice was serious, his face set in stone. "We're getting married."

At his declaration, a loud ringing noise pierced through the air. "Fuck, what now?" Leo said, his tone terse.

Augustus swayed over to the desk and picked up his phone. "Yes, Adonis," he answered while staring at us. "I'm actually happy you called; I need help with—"

Augustus's face fell. "No, I guess… But when? Fine. They don't need to send the guard to bring me in. Right. I'll be there."

When he set the phone down, his eyes scanned the room. "The lords have summoned me for a special meeting in three days. They're demanding a paternity test."

Chapter Seventeen

"August?" I said while working my way up to the guest bedroom. I'd given him plenty of time to sober up and wanted to see if he was okay. Our engagement felt rushed and anticlimactic. We'd never really taken the time to court one another or explore our romance. Even though I knew that I loved him, the entire engagement felt cheapened because of all the obstacles against us.

I slowly opened the bedroom door and saw August lying on the ruffled bed where I'd just had sex with Atticus the night before. He wore gray sweatpants slung low on his hips, and his hand was placed over his head.

The bed's frame was made of pockmarked wood,

and the feathers inside the mattress were so thin that I knew it wasn't very comfortable.

"You okay?" I asked softly, worried I'd spook him.

He slowly opened his eyes and looked at me. "No. I'm not okay."

I moved toward him, putting my hand on the bed and touching his leg. "Do you want to talk about it?" I asked.

He shook his head. "I fucked up," he said.

"Fucked up?" I asked. "What did you do?"

He sat up. "It's what I didn't do," he said. "I didn't get the chance to take you on romantic dates. I didn't propose like I wanted to—like you deserved. I didn't do any of the bullshit romantic gestures chicks love."

I rolled my eyes. "Calling romantic gestures *bullshit* kind of takes away from the magic of it."

August smiled. "That's fair," he said. "But even with all of these fuckups, you're still willing to marry me."

"Because I love you."

His expression changed and the smile left his face. "Are you sure?"

"That I love you?" I asked.

He nodded. "You're not doing it just because you think you have to, right?"

I shook my head vigorously. "No."

"It's a big deal," he said. "I want you to be really,

really sure. Because if you do this, if you marry me, it's for the rest of your life. And you can't undo it. You can't get an annulment after all of the stuff that's happened. You can't divorce me when you decide I don't deserve you," he said. "What I mean to say," he added quickly, "is that…I want you to know that I love you. I want to prove to you that I love you every single day. I want to marry you, Christine. More than anything. But not like this. Not because my mother was blackmailing you. Not because Lord Nathan is breathing down my neck. I want to marry you because…" He paused then smiled. "I want to marry you because when we were kids, you stole a slice of apple cheesecake for me."

I bursted out laughing. "Your mother was so mad. I had to hide it behind my back."

He grabbed my hands. "I want to marry you because when we were thirteen, you tackled me in the garden and tickled me after I got grounded for flipping off a priest."

Another laugh escaped me. "I still remember how he prayed for your soul as you threw your middle finger up." We locked eyes and I licked my lips. "Do you want to know why I want to marry you, August?"

"Tell me, love."

My reasoning was more than words, more than anything I could ever express. August was like home.

Warmth. A memory of happier times. He represented my naivety and innocence. A place where I'd never have to have my guard up. A place where I knew I wouldn't be judged for anything I did. "Because when I see you, I feel settled. I feel…safe. I want to marry you because I want to start a family with you. I want to grow old with you, August. I want to travel and see the world with you. I want to go to the beach with you and plant roses with you and go to amusement parks. I want to sit by a fire with you and hold your hand. I want to fight with you and laugh with you and live with you."

We stared at each other in silence. He was shirtless and full of tension, the dips of his abs flexing as he processed my words. The way he looked at me made me feel like nothing else in the world existed. August had always craved validation. He needed it like air, and I wanted him to know exactly where I stood.

I continued. "I want to marry you because you remind me of my family," I said. "We had our ups and downs. But the truth is, you're my best friend. This is what we are. You're the person I've always longed for. When I feel like I'm losing control and death is creeping up on me and darkness is surrounding me, you light the way. I want to marry you because you give me life, August."

I could see the tears in his eyes when he reached out

to me. He wrapped me in his arms. "I want to marry you for many reasons," he said. "When I say that I want to marry you, I'm saying I want to marry you for *you*. Not the girl I knew back then. Not the fighter you've become. You. All of you. Every last bit of the things that make you who you are." He kissed me, his hands cupping my face. "I want to marry you because you make me happy. Because you're everything I've ever wanted, everything I've ever needed. I want to marry you because when I kiss you, I feel my soul shift. I feel a calmness, a peace that hasn't been there for a very long time. Like I've found a part of me that was lost. You make me feel stronger than I've ever been. Stronger than I've ever thought I could be. You pull out the best in me. You make me a better person—a better man." He wiped the tears from my eyes. "I want to marry you because you're my everything."

I drank in the sight of him, looking at his bare chest, his sharp jawline covered in dark stubble making him look rugged, so sexy. We stared at one another for a long moment, processing our declarations. Then, he leaned in slowly, brushing his lips against mine with a featherlight touch. I could feel his body shake against my chest as he held me, but that was all I felt. His body shook, but he didn't move. He didn't kiss me. He just hovered, transfixed.

I moved my hands to the back of his neck, pulling his face closer. I made my lips open, forcing the wall between us to dissolve into nothingness. He grabbed my waist while I pulled him closer, kissing him like no one else existed.

I kissed him.

I kissed him voraciously. Lovingly. Fiercely.

He kissed me back and it was fire and passion. It was the two of us in a bubble, the old and the new, mixing together so seamlessly. I moaned and fisted his hair, making the kiss deeper. He pressed me to the thin mattress, running his hands down my back until they landed on my ass. He squeezed and I whimpered, arching my back to give him better access.

"I love you," he said before pulling away and looking down at me. He pressed his forehead to mine and whispered, "I love you, and I feel like I don't deserve you. I can't have a relationship unless I know you forgive me," he said between kisses. "I need to know you're with me, Christine. I need to know you trust me."

I kissed him again. "Forgive you? For what?"

"For not chasing after you. For not being the man you deserve."

"I wished you would see yourself the way I see you," I replied. "I trust you. I *love* you." He continued kissing me, pressing me into the mattress. His kisses were desperate and hungry. "There's nothing to forgive, August. We can't change the past." I brought my hands to his cheeks and made his face turn to mine. "I do trust you. With my life."

He kissed me then, passionately. Our hands were everywhere. We were so eager to touch one another that it made my head spin.

I could feel him getting hard. His erection pressed against my thigh. I rubbed myself against him. I needed him inside me. I needed to feel him, to experience him. I helped him with my shirt, lifting it over my head before he covered my neck with wet, sloppy kisses. My heart was racing with anticipation.

August needed to be loved in a way where I was all his. Where there was no questioning. It was unconditional. Even if I shared my heart with others, this with just us was a connection that was insurmountable and true.

August buried his face in my neck, kissing and sucking on my skin, smelling me and claiming me. August's sweat was a strange combination of musk and pine and something else I couldn't place. His skin always smelled like it had a hint of expensive cologne, and it made my mouth water.

He grabbed my bra strap, pulling it down my

shoulder and exposing me. "I need you. I need this," he said. "I need to feel you, love. I need to feel you around me." He continued kissing my neck while he unclasped my bra, his hands shaking. He pulled it off, exposing my breasts. He was so gentle with them, and I sighed at his soothing touch.

He kissed my right breast, sucking my nipple into his mouth, tugging it between his lips. I arched my back and he stopped kissing, holding my breast and taking in a deep breath. Then he kissed my nipple again, flicking his tongue across it and making me scream. My body flushed with heat. This was the August I knew. Tender. Sweet.

Once we were both completely naked, he left a trail of kisses down my body and pried open my legs, staring at my pussy like it was God's gift to man. "Look how pretty you are," he mused.

"August," I panted. I wanted him to taste me. To eat me, to drink me. To make me his.

He kissed my inner thigh, flicking his tongue out and making me giggle. "I missed you," he whispered. Then he grabbed my thighs and pulled me toward him, splaying my legs open so he had full access. When he kissed the top of my thigh, I growled.

He dragged his tongue across my pussy and tasted me, blowing a hot breath over my wet skin. I shivered and gasped when his mouth made contact with me, his tongue licking me like an ice cream cone. He slid a finger inside me while he sucked on my clit, his other hand on my knee, holding me still. He was relentless.

My body was going wild. I closed my eyes and felt every nerve ending in my body come alive. I could feel him inside me, on me, over me, as if we were one.

He removed his finger, then drove his tongue into me, and I grabbed a handful of his hair, pulling hard. He tasted me deep before pulling his tongue out and sucking on my clit, moving his lips and tongue quickly. I felt the pressure building in the pit of my stomach, my hips bucking. He continued sucking and licking before reaching a finger up to my clit and gently rubbing it in a circle.

August then kissed my pussy again, taking in a deep breath as he pressed his tongue against my clit. He licked me, slowly and deliberately. He licked my clit like it was the most delicate thing in the world, and I protested, gripping the sheets and arching my back. "I need…I need…"

"I know, love. I know," he whispered against my clit before working me harder. Faster.

He licked and sucked, stroked and toyed with me. I could feel his finger working inside me, and it thrilled me to know he could taste how turned on I was. I was so wet and so slippery. I wanted him to feel this, to know what he was doing to me.

I came like a bomb, hard and dangerous, and August kept licking me through every wave of pleasure. I could feel the walls of my pussy pulsing, desire flooding me.

He looked up at me, smiling. He loved it when I came. He loved to watch me, and the way his eyes lit up when he heard me cry out made me feel like the luckiest girl in the world. He raised up and kissed me. He licked my neck and sucked on my nipples, pushing me back into the bed. I tasted myself on his tongue.

I arched my back, pressing my hips into his. He grabbed my hips and kissed me deeper.

Starvation.

It was all I felt.

Starvation for August.

I grabbed his face and kissed him, stroking his cheek. I kissed him again and again, desperate for his touch, needing it.

He pulled away and looked at me, his eyes sparkling. He ran his hand over my thigh, and I let go of his face and ran my fingers through his hair. August captivated me with his eyes, and I closed mine, letting myself get lost in him. My body was aching, begging for him.

His hand brushed my pussy. "Baby, please," I begged. "I need you."

He grinned, biting his bottom lip. He tried to stifle his chuckle, but it caused my body to shake.

He pushed his cock between my thighs, rubbing my clit. He rubbed my clit harder. "That's it, sweetheart. Make that pretty little pussy good and wet for me."

I was already soaking. Desperate. Dying for him.

August brushed my clit with his cock and moaned. He was teasing me, and it was driving me crazy. "Please, August. I want to feel you inside me."

He leaned forward and kissed me, rubbing my clit harder. I could feel my orgasm building, the knot in my stomach tightening. I wiggled my hips, trying to relieve the pressure building there.

"Don't you dare come again yet, love," he whispered against my ear.

I closed my eyes, relaxing my hips and trying hard not to come. I wanted to obey him. I wanted to shatter on his command. "Please," I begged. "Please take me, August."

He grinned. "You asked so nicely." He grabbed my hips and pushed himself inside me, groaning in my ear. Then he pulled out slowly, his hand on my chest, holding me still. He kissed me again and pushed himself inside me, my pussy strangling his dick. He muttered, "So tight."

I wrapped my legs around his waist, holding onto him and kissing him like my life depended on it. He moved faster, his eyes on my face as he watched me take him. He made me feel wild and feral, greedy for him and what we had.

The feeling intensified as he fucked me faster, groaning. He grabbed my breast and squeezed, then reached down and tugged on my clit until it hurt, like a pinch of pleasure. "I'm going to come," I moaned. "August, I'm going to come."

"No," he said sharply. "You're not."

My body was shaking, my toes curling as my orgasm grew closer. I knew there was no way I could hold off.

"You're not going to. You're going to stay right on the edge. Just like this. Feel that torture, love." He let out a shaky breath. "This sweet torture." And he was right. If I hadn't already come on his face, I would have been frustrated. When he toyed with me like this, the release was ten times more intense. And it was all because he wanted it that way.

"Please," I begged, my breath coming out in pants. "I want to come."

He shook his head and smiled. "I missed you, love.

Thought you were dead. So I'm going to take my fucking time with you."

I bucked my hips.

"You're so responsive." He pumped into me faster and harder, then started circling my clit with his thumb. I could feel his dick throbbing inside me, and I clenched my pussy over him. I needed to come. It was unbearable. He was going to kill me.

"I love you," I begged. "Please, August."

"Shh." He stroked my hair. "You're going to get your wish, love. I'm going to let you come."

I didn't move. I just stayed there in my torture, wrapped up in him. I was desperate. I wanted to explode.

I cried out, unable to hold it in. I wept. I screamed. August held me as my body shuddered, the orgasm ripping through me. It was so strong that I grabbed my own hair and pulled.

I yelled out, trying to catch my breath.

But August wasn't done yet.

"See, love? I'm a benevolent king. Giving you just what you asked for." He grabbed my ass and slowly fucked me, making sure his cock hit every nerve in its path. I was frantic with desire. He pulled out slowly and grabbed himself, stroking his cock. "You look so fucking hot like that. I'll never get enough of this." He pushed back inside me.

The pressure was building once more, and I knew there was no way in hell I'd be able to stop a third orgasm. I was too sensitive. Too full of him.

"Fuck," he hissed, picking up the pace. His moans were like thunder; the way he growled was pure sex.

"Oh, God," I murmured. "Don't stop."

"I'm not going to. I can't. You feel too good, love." He looked at me, his eyes soft and full of desire. He pushed himself into me deeper, and my pussy clenched around his cock.

I sobbed, the demand building in my stomach. It was all I could think about.

August.

Feeling him inside me.

Losing myself in him.

He grunted, his grip tightening on my ass. "That's it, love."

My body trembled, my back arching, my legs shaking. Another orgasm was coming, and I couldn't stop it.

He grunted and grabbed my hips, pounding me hard. His grip was tight, his strokes hard.

August let his head fall back. I could see the pleasure on his face. "You...fuck. You're so good. God, baby." Then he looked at me, his eyes sparkling. I could see he was close. He thrust quickly, groaning. "You're so fucking sexy. You're going to make me come. You're going to make me fucking come."

"Yes," I gasped.

August came hard, shoving himself deep inside me. When he came, he moaned. His face was tight, his lips parted. I clenched my pussy, wanting to milk him of every drop he had. "That's it, baby," he whispered. "That's it." He kept thrusting until his orgasm was over.

He collapsed on top of me and kissed my neck. "I'm still so fucking hard for you. We could do this for days and it wouldn't be enough." He kissed my cheek and pulled out of me, his cock dripping wet.

I turned my head and looked at him, smiling. "You'll have the rest of your life to do this."

He laughed and leaned in, kissing me slowly. "Give me fucking eternity, love."

Chapter Eighteen

The next day, when I came down for breakfast, Leo was flipping pancakes with his shirt off. I could see every defined muscle, the tense raise of his shoulders. Atticus had all the utilities turned on the night he found me, and I was thankful we could stay here with everything we needed. I was in domestic bliss, but Leo's sour mood made it difficult to enjoy it too much.

The scowl on his face made me sad, but I didn't know how to fix things between us.

I knew I looked like I'd been thoroughly fucked. August and I were at it all night. He was insatiable, fucking me the way he went through life—with reckless abandon.

"Food is almost ready," he said in a terse tone. I poured myself a cup of coffee and sat down, forcing myself not to feel bad for last night.

"Are you okay?" I asked. Just because I was going to live without shame didn't mean I was heartless. I could practically feel his anger burning as hot as the skillet.

He didn't answer, and more words tumbled out of me. "You seem tense—"

"Don't, I'm fine. You don't owe me anything."

"Leo. Please don't be like this."

That's when he stopped mid-flip, and he turned and stared at me. His eyes were bloodshot and tired and his mouth pulled into a frown. I could see little crescent marks on his thighs as if he spent the night gripping his legs in anger.

"I'm gonna go put a shirt on," he said before sliding the pancake onto a plate and turning off the stove. His body was a work of art, and I wanted to run my hands down the inside of his thighs and let my mouth trace trails down his spine.

"I wouldn't be mad if you didn't," I said with a flirty smirk. He could be grumpy all he wanted, but I knew I'd have to push past his walls.

"Didn't you get enough last night?" he spat angrily.

I stood up and made my way over to him. He leaned against the counter with wide eyes and a heaving chest. "You can be mad at me all you want." I trailed a finger down his chest. "I'm being selfish, I know. And you don't understand it." I lifted up on my toes to whisper in his ear. "But I want you too."

He let out a shaky breath. "You're gonna be the death of me, you know that?" he said, his voice hoarse.

"I know," I said, resting my head against his chest. I'd pushed him too far, too fast and I knew it. He placed his hand on the back of my head, and I swore I felt his heart thudding against the palm of my hand. I pushed myself up to kiss him, and he pressed his forehead against mine. "I'm sorry," I whispered.

He ran his hand through my hair and kissed me longer than before.

"Stop this. We can't do this."

"Why not?" I asked.

"Because it's not right," he said.

"It feels right to me," I said.

"No, I mean, if we start, it can't end well for either of us."

"One of these days, Leo, you'll stop pushing our girl away," Atticus said while strolling into the kitchen. His button-up shirt was undone and his pants hung low on his hips. He smiled at me and I reluctantly pulled away from Leo to greet him. "Morning, Little Monster," he said before kissing me. His lips were minty.

"Morning." It felt strange to flutter from one to the other, but also so fucking right.

"Did you have a good night?"

A deep blush coated my cheeks. "Yes."

Atticus grinned. "Good. Because if it wasn't, I was going to slit Augustus's throat."

I swallowed nervously.

His attention turned to Leo, and he walked over to him. He placed his hand on Leo's shoulder, and all of a sudden, Leo closed his eyes and tensed. Atticus made a show of squeezing, and all of Leo's muscles bulged and strained, like they were fighting to get free. Atticus's touch held a weight to it that I couldn't fathom. Seeing them together made my stomach twist, but it wasn't unpleasant.

"You're tense," he said, pulling his hand away.

Leo rubbed his face. "I'm fine."

"No, you're not," Atticus said. He placed his hand on Leo's chest. "Why don't you go spend some time with Christine today, Leo? We can't move forward with the wedding until we announce she's alive at the meeting with the lords, and she needs someone to keep her occupied."

Leo scowled. "I have things to do."

Atticus cocked a brow. "I wasn't asking."

"I don't take orders from you."

"But you're just so good at it," Atticus goaded.

Leo smacked his hand out of the way, and Atticus's smile faltered. "Enough," he said. "I have a job to do. You and August might be okay with sharing her, but I'm not. I'm here, I'm helping. But I'm not going to let you fuck around with my feelings. It's hard enough without you making innuendos."

"You'd be so much happier if you gave in, Leo." Atticus's eyes blazed. "Christine wants you, and I want whatever makes my Little Monster happy. So you can take what you *both* want. Or I can command you."

Leo glared back. "I'm not afraid of you."

Atticus snorted in amusement. "Leo, you've been afraid you're whole fucking life. It's why you suit up. It's not to protect the Crown or Christine. It's to prove yourself." Atticus stopped and cocked his head to the side. "I just wonder, what's got you so scared?"

"Fuck off," Leo grunted before shoving past him and disappearing in a flash.

"Leo isn't like August, Atticus. You can't bully him into doing what you want. He's...gentle. Tender."

Atticus scoffed. "That man isn't gentle. I bet if he stopped being so terrified of the truth, he'd be the most ruthless out of all of us. He just needs some guidance."

I arched a brow. "And are you going to be the one to guide him?"

He bowed before grabbing the plate of pancakes. "If it's what my queen wishes." He then plopped down at the table and started eating.

I stared after Leo, and my stomach began to churn. Should I go after him? Was I making this worse? I sat down at the table and Atticus pushed the plate of pancakes in front of me before giving me a searching look. "What's wrong?"

"Nothing." I grabbed a pancake, but I wasn't hungry.

"Are you sure?"

"Yeah."

He watched me, but I pretended not to notice. I tried to swallow my food, but it tasted like cardboard.

Atticus sighed. "Go after him, Little Monster."

"Are you sure? I know I was with August last night and—"

"And I stroked myself to the sound of your screams," he said, cutting me off.

My mouth popped open. Atticus seemed so…calm about this. It was almost too good to be true. "Are you sure?" I asked for the second time.

"Little Monster, when I need you, I'll demand your time. I'll claim your cunt. I'll spread you wide on this kitchen table and lick you clean. I'm not afraid to steal whatever time I need, so you don't need to worry about my feelings on the matter. I'll make sure I get whatever we both need. Go. To. Him."

I leaned across the table to kiss him, then stood up.

It was time to find Leo.

* * *

I found him sitting on the couch, his arms spread out across the back. His eyes were closed, but I could see the tension in his shoulders.

I hesitated, unsure of what to say or do. "Hey," I said softly. He opened his eyes but didn't move. "Can we talk?"

He huffed a laugh and shook his head. "I don't know." He leaned forward, resting his elbows on his knees. "Atticus seems to think he knows everything about me. Why don't you talk to him?"

I bit my bottom lip. "It seems he struck a nerve."

Leo's face twisted as he scowled back. "He didn't strike a nerve. I'm annoyed. That's it." I didn't believe him.

"What are you afraid of?" My voice wavered and my heart sank as I watched Leo's shoulders slump.

"You," he said.

"Me?" I asked, shocked.

Leo scrubbed his face with his hands. "Yes. You. You hit all the buttons, Christine. You make me feel things I shouldn't. I shouldn't like you."

"Why?"

He ran his hand through his long blond hair. "My dad left my mom, you know. When I was young. She was pregnant with my sister. He'd always been a mean bastard but hid behind his perfect middle-class family and a smile. Would mentally abuse her. Called her fat. Said she was worthless. Found a hot, young flight attendant and just forgot about his family."

I swallowed. "That must've been hard." I knew his father wasn't in the picture, but wasn't aware of the specifics.

"Yeah. It was. My mom fell into a deep depression and lost herself. I felt responsible for her. For my sister. We had no money and I had to join the guard to send them my paychecks."

"You were a kid, too," I said. "It wasn't your responsibility to make up for your shitty father."

"If I didn't step up, then who would?"

"I'm so sorry." I didn't know what to say.

"I hated him. I hated him so much. I was angry at what he did to my mom. I wanted to hurt him. The stupid, arrogant bastard ruined my family." Leo's gaze burned with an intensity I'd never seen before. "I decided love wasn't really worth it. I used to treat women like shit. I decided to fuck around as much as I could."

I nodded and he continued speaking.

"Then I joined the guard. I stopped caring. I stopped feeling. I stopped trying. I was just going through the motions. But then you came along. You were sweet and innocent, and you made me feel. You made me want something I couldn't have. I'm terrified of another man touching you. I'm afraid to fall in love with you, because I know what I'll do to anyone who hurts you. I'd rip them to shreds without a second thought. And I don't want to be that person."

"You're not a monster, Leo," I said, but I shivered at the way his voice was so cold. "You're not like *me*." Was that his true fear? Giving into his demons and letting loose the rage in his soul? I'd never seen him like this before.

"That's what he calls you, right? Little Monster. Well, here's the truth, Christine. The people that let their rage out are actually safer. They're predictable. It's the people like me—the ones that lock it up tight and never let it out—that you should fear more. Because eventually, we break. Eventually, we ruin everything we love. Eventually, we leave."

"You're not going to leave me, Leo. And I'm not leaving you," I said softly.

He groaned and grabbed his head. "You don't get it. I'm already gone. Every time I look at you, I'm lost. I'm lost in you." He looked up at me, his eyes filled with raw hunger. "I'm scared of you. I'm scared of what you do to me."

"You don't need to be scared. I'm not going anywhere." I reached out and grabbed his hand, but he was too far away. I walked to him. I needed to be closer. I needed him to feel me.

I leaned over and grabbed his hand. I placed it on my chest, right over my heart.

Leo's breath blew out of his lips, and I saw the struggle in his eyes.

"Do you feel that?" I asked.

His eyes searched mine. "Yes," he whispered.

"My heart, Leo. That's yours. I'm not taking it back."

"Christine." He sounded defeated. "I'm afraid of this. I'm afraid of loving you. What if one day you choose them?"

"Your heart is safe with me, Leo," I whispered. "I'll never hurt you."

Leo shuddered and grabbed me, pulling me into his lap. He didn't say anything, but his silence spoke volumes. He was letting me in. He was letting me in, and I could feel the difference in him already.

Yes, he was still terrified, but he was letting me fight his demons.

"Let me love you, Leo," I whispered. "Let me fight for you. Let me be yours."

He shook his head, but I kissed him. He didn't protest. I unraveled him and showed him what love felt like. I showed him what being cared for felt like.

I could feel it.

My heart was his.

My soul was his.

I was his.

And he was mine.

I loved him.

And I'd never let him go.

I loved him.

I loved *all* of them.

My heart might have been battered and bruised, but it still had the capacity to love big. And each thudding beat was for the three men who owned me.

Chapter Nineteen

ATTICUS

My fingers pulled at the corset wrapped tightly around her creamy skin, pushing her plump breasts up so that they were like plush pillows for my chin. I wanted to lick every inch of her, savor the taste. But we had appearances to make. Men to kill. Thrones to steal.

The corset clung to her skin like a candle flame, each silver thread perfectly woven in place. The satin finish was smooth, shimmering as she breathed.

"I still don't think it's a good idea to bring her," Augustus said from the bed. He was watching Christine brace her hands against the bedpost. Her willowy body was bent over as she sucked in and I laced her up. I knew corsets were a damned contraption, and there was something so beautiful about seeing my Little Monster free and soft. But I also liked knowing she was wrapped up tight like a present for me.

"They won't believe she's alive otherwise," I said as a slight moan escaped her lips. She had thick lace garters on her thighs and, fuck, I wanted to dig my teeth into her ass.

"And what if Lord Nathan claims her right then and there?" Augustus asked.

"Then I'll put a bullet through his skull." I spun Christine around and dragged my thumb along her lip. "You had a crumb."

Her tongue snaked out to brush against my skin. Cheeky. "You'll shoot him in front of all the lords?"

"You think I'll let him harm you?" I wrapped my hands around her neck and pulled her close. "You're safe with me, Little Monster."

I pulled Christine to me, my hand still around her throat. Her pussy was wet. I could smell her desire. Her trust. And, God, it was intoxicating.

I kissed her hard and fast, then pushed her away. Augustus cleared his throat. "Enough with the macho act. We all know you'll torture and kill anyone who looks at her wrong." He waved his hand in annoyance, but I saw the way his eyes narrowed when I touched Christine.

I was testing him. If we were ever going to be comfortable about this, we couldn't hide. Quiet little fucks in the dark while we all tiptoed around the situation wasn't doing anyone any good.

I shrugged. "I just like to make my intentions known."

Christine's gaze darted between us, but she was silent. Meek. I knew she was holding back. I'd seen her anger, seen her take on an entire army of men by herself. I'd seen the flash of strength in her eyes as she stood, tall and proud, in front of the lords.

She didn't know how to be quiet.

And I'd be damned if I let her be quiet with us.

If she was going to stand by me, she had to be strong. She had to show the lords she wasn't a shy little thing. She was a fierce ruler, sweet…and deadly.

"Where is Leo?" I asked before finding the diamond necklace I'd bought her. She'd waltz into that room full of lords looking like a damn queen.

"I was just getting her dress," he said while walking into the bedroom. His eyes lingered on Christine's legs before he tossed the garment bag onto the bed beside Augustus. "Did you really have to pick something so…so…"

"Sexy?" I finished for him. "Powerful?"

"Revealing," he said, his lips set in a grim line.

"Let me see," Augustus said before unzipping the bag. He let out a low whistle. "Interesting choice, Atticus."

Her hair was curled and pinned on the nape of her neck. The necklace I bought her would delicately brush her chest, and the diamond studs in her ears sparkled. Her breasts were pushed up high, the tops peeking out from the top of her corset. Once she put on the formfitting black dress with the slit up her thigh, all eyes would be on her.

Christine's eyes were wide and uncertain while she stood by the bed. She held the dress against her body and moved to the floor-length mirror. "The royal publicist will have a field day," she mused.

"This dress was made for you," Augustus said, his eyes roving over the beautiful creature that was my Little Monster.

A roll of her eyes. "You just like it because it shows off all my best assets. Those grumpy old men will have a heart attack when they see me."

She twisted her body, trying to look at her back.

"Don't be ridiculous," I said to her. "You look like a queen."

"But—"

"No buts." I slid my hand up her thigh, gripping the fabric of the dress, then digging for her skin. "This dress is meant for you."

"Yes, it is," she said softly.

I spun her around and the dress fell from her fingertips onto the floor. My mouth found hers, and soon I was kissing her softly and fiercely. She seemed tense in my arms. I knew she was aware of the two men watching us. Even though she was strong in demanding what she wanted, she wasn't invincible. I could feel the guilt in every sweep of her tongue, every muted moan. She wasn't giving me her all, and that simply wasn't acceptable.

"Are you afraid to kiss me in front of them?" I whispered.

Augustus cleared his throat. "We don't have time for this."

Leo clenched his fist. "I'm not standing here and watching," he added before turning to leave. Leo's face was twisted in anger, but his eyes were soft. His breathing was labored from desire.

I sighed and pulled the gun that was holstered on my hip out, aiming it at Leo. "You're going to stay."

His eyes widened in shock. "You going to fucking shoot me if I don't sit here and watch you get off?"

I smiled. Christine was stiff against me, her mouth

parted. But the shiver that went down her spine told me she *liked* the violence. She liked that I was willing to bash some heads to get us all to work together.

"That's exactly what I'm going to do," I said.

"Atticus," she rasped.

"This is so fucked up," Augustus groaned, but his tone was heavy with eagerness. I could hear how much he was enjoying this with every rough breath he took.

"You're going to let go, Little Monster. You're going to kiss me. Please me. And they're going to watch, or I'll shoot your little shadow. You don't want his brains splattered all over the room, do you?"

She timidly shook her head. "No."

"Good. So kiss me like you fucking mean it."

Her hand moved to my chest, then to my jaw. The other massaged my lower back, desperate. She moaned, the sound vibrating against my tongue. Pulling her closer, her body against mine, I slipped my hand over her hip, cupping the curve of her ass. My fingers dug in, pulling her to me so that her breasts were crushed against my chest. I kissed her hungrily, possessively.

My Little Monster belonged to me.

Leo raged as he watched us. My arm burned as I aimed the gun at him, my finger hovering over the trigger. Christine dropped to her knees and fumbled with my buckle.

"I fucking hate you." Leo's jaw clenched.

"You like taking orders," I told him. Her fingertips brushed my cock, teasing me. "This is all your fault," I told him. "If you'd just accept things, I wouldn't have to threaten you."

"I'll kill you," he choked out. The sight of Christine on her knees was getting to him.

"Keep talking and I'll shove the barrel down your throat. You can suck eternity while she sucks me off." Christine's lips brushed against me, my cock springing to life. I held her hair back and looked down at her, watching her lips wrap around my thick shaft. I closed my eyes and groaned. She took my cock deep, her lips pulling tight while she bobbed her head. "That's it, Little Monster. Suck it good and hard. I want this tight little throat."

"Holy shit, Atticus," Augustus groaned.

Leo was still seething. "You're fucked up," he said, his voice low.

I chuckled and tilted my head back. Her tongue caressed my balls. "Are you enjoying the show?"

"No," he lied. Christine shifted and opened her mouth, sucking my cock in deep again. I kneaded her hair, tugging her head back, then forward.

"Fuck," I choked out. The pleasure of her mouth was almost too much to bear. She was pulling at me.

Guiding me. Tasting me. The sensation of her lips and tongue was driving me insane. I was shaking. I didn't have control anymore. *She owned me.* "Christine."

She stroked me, her fingertips brushing against my velvet skin. I could feel myself losing control. I was going to come in her mouth. It was going to be glorious.

"Fuck," Leo said quietly, his eyes wide.

The gun fell from my hand and clattered to the floor. "Yes, Little Monster," I groaned. "Slide your mouth up and down my cock. Take it deep."

"Atticus," she whispered. Her mouth was warm and wet.

"Like that, Little Monster?" I asked her. "Like sucking the cock that owns you?"

Her hand stroked me, her tongue teasing my tip. My eyes locked on hers. I could see how torn she was, how much she wanted to please me but still felt ashamed.

"Stop thinking," I said to her. "You're a strong, powerful woman. You're mine. I'm *your* king right now."

Her fingers slid between her legs, and she began to play with herself, moaning against my cock. Leaning back, she began to rub her clit, her cries loud and desperate.

"That's it," I murmured. "Show them who's in charge. Remember who you belong to."

Leo watched her, his expression torn between hunger and anger. He couldn't take his eyes off her.

I stroked her hair, watching as she pleasured herself and pumped me with her mouth, her groans growing louder with each pass of her fingers over her clit. I could feel my cock throb with each beat of her heart. My balls tightened, aching for release.

"You're so fucking wet, Little Monster," I told her.

I stood tall, then grabbed her by her hair, the other hand firmly on her head. I pumped into her mouth and she writhed while she took it.

"Christine," I said savagely. "Christine, Christine, Christine. Tell me who loves you."

"You," she mumbled, her mouth full and those beautiful eyes searching mine. She ground her hips into her hand, her body on fire. I could tell she was close to coming.

"Fuck yeah," I groaned. "You're going to make me come in your mouth, Little Monster."

She rubbed her clit faster and faster.

"There you go. You know what you fucking want," I told her. She looked so beautiful, so submissive. I could see nothing else but the object of my desire. Everything else was distant.

"That's it," I gasped. "You know what to do. You know what to make me feel. Suck me, Little Monster."

Her hand shifted and she slid a finger deep inside herself. Her lips clenched around my shaft, and I groaned. The sight was so amazing I could barely keep my eyes open. She was everything I could imagine and more.

She sucked, her hand stroking me up and down, then gripping me tight. I held her against me and felt my release. It was as if every ounce of my energy was leaving my body. "There it is. There it fucking is. This is all for you. All for you, baby." I felt light. Free. Liberated. I felt alive and invincible. Nothing could kill me. Nothing could tear me down. I thrust into her mouth and she swallowed me down, again and again.

Then she came even harder than I did, as if watching me unravel released her own pleasure. Her body shook while she came. I could feel her squirm and shiver, her thighs squeezing together. A strangely delicate gasp escaped her lips. I loved the sound. I wanted to record it and play it on repeat.

She sat back on her calves, letting go of my cock. Her chest was heaving, as were her hips. She was riding her orgasm, strumming her clit hard, all while she watched me, her eyes glassy and lips parted. She was so beautiful and so willing. Her orgasm went on for what seemed like forever, then she let out a long, slow moan. Her body relaxed, her hips rocking gently, her fingertips fluttering over that needy nub as she enjoyed the very last drop of bliss.

And when it was all done, she was kneeling on the floor, with my cum running down her chin, looking like a fucking queen. She licked her lips and smiled up at me.

"Good girl," I said. Her eyes were wide and adoring. She grabbed my hand and kissed my palm, then looked up at me, her eyes like a doe's. "Did you like that, Little Monster?" I asked, my voice hoarse.

"Mmm…" She trailed off, still in a daze. I wanted to eat her out, but we didn't have a lot of time.

I tucked my dick back into my pants and buttoned them before bending down to pick up the gun. Both Leo and Augustus were staring at us.

I waved the gun. "You had a chance to leave," I said with a laugh. I was giving him an out. Proving a point. Leo Winthrop didn't leave, because he *wanted* to be here.

"Fuck me. I just watched my brother get a blow job," Augustus said before wrinkling his nose. "Is that fucked up? I'm hard as a rock. The royal therapist is going to have a long chat with me. I need a drink."

"No drinks," Christine said.

"Do you take anything fucking serious, Augustus?" Leo yelled. "We're fucking around when we should be getting ready for the most important meeting of our lives. This is stupid and exactly why we shouldn't be doing this. It's a distraction. It's going to end badly."

Christine stood up on wobbly legs, shame and tears filling her eyes.

"Oh, I don't know why you're so fucking serious. I'm fucking hard as a rock. I don't know how this is going to work, but watching Christine do *that* was an eye opener for sure," Augustus said with a smile.

"Fantastic," Christine mumbled.

Leo smacked the top of his forehead. "Fuck you. Fuck *all* of you."

Now that just wouldn't do.

I surged forward, the gun still in my hand. Shoving Leo against the wall, I placed the barrel against his temple in one swift move.

"You don't talk to her like that," I growled.

"I hate you," he whispered, his face darkening in rage.

I could see the hatred in his eyes. He was trying to hold it together. He was trying to talk his way out of this. He was trying to ignore his feelings. "You do it again, and I'm going to put a bullet through your brain, understand?" I said slowly. "You don't make her feel bad for taking what she wants. You don't make her feel shame or guilt. I won't stand for it."

"I hate you," he choked out once more, his throat constricting.

"I know you do," I said, digging the barrel deeper. "But I'm pressed against you right now, and you know what I feel, Leo?"

"Fuck you," he said, his eyes on fire.

"You're hard as a fucking rock. So you may hate me, but you liked seeing her suck me off. You *love* her." He said nothing. "I saw it in your eyes when you were watching, didn't I?" I growled. "I bet you're imagining it."

He swallowed. "Imagining what?"

"Both of us with her. Her creamy skin. Hands roaming her body. Both our cocks sliding in and out of her dripping pussy." Christine's breath hitched. Oh, my Little Monster liked that visual. "You feel it. I know you do."

"I'm not feeling anything."

"You're wrong," I said, my lips close to his ear. His breathing was shallow. "You're feeling it right now, aren't you?" I asked, stepping back and looking at him. "Feel that, huh? Feel that power that you crave. It's mine. It's always been mine. And if you play nice, I'll share."

"Shut up!" he roared. I grabbed the collar of his shirt and glared at him.

"*You* shut up, Leo." I pulled him forward, dragging him to the floor. I placed the gun to his temple again as my brother and Christine stared at me, neither of them saying a word. This had to happen. It was the only way. "There's a lot more at stake than the Crown. This"—I pounded the floor with my fist—"isn't going to be some lighthearted thing. This is going to change your life. Your world. This is going to ruin you. It's going to ruin everything. And it'll *all* be worth it."

His face was red with rage. His muscles were tight. I could feel them twisting underneath my touch.

"Even if you did hate me, Leo, there's a part of you that loves her, that wants to protect her. You want to know what it feels like to have your hands on her. To have her soft body pressed against you. To have her against you with her hands in your hair. You want to feel her lips on yours."

Slowly, I let him go and backed away from him, the gun still aimed at his head. He pushed himself off the ground and glared at me, his hands clenched into fists.

I leaned forward. "You're mad at me for fucking your girl, but you're even madder that you didn't join us."

And with those words, I left the room.

Chapter Twenty

CHRISTINE

The limousine crawled up the gravel drive, flanked on either side by a line of sentries in dark green uniforms, holding rifles at the ready. It was a sight that felt wrong, a reminder of times long past, before technology and convenience had rendered the military obsolete in this world. I wondered how much longer these men would be expected to stand guard at this gate, a relic of a bygone age. With all the threats at the king's door, it made sense that they'd revert to something familiar. Armed men in uniform were a deterrent.

Or at least, they hoped they were.

The smoke still lingered in the air, forming a pall

above us like a funeral shroud. I had grown accustomed to smog over my years of living in this city, but this was something altogether different. This smoke was the product of destruction, a reminder of the upheaval we had all just experienced.

The soldier on the gate stepped forward and opened the door of the limo, ushering us into the palace grounds. I stepped out and stood before the large gate, barely able to take it all in. Before me stood an imposing facade, its ornate turrets and statues standing silhouetted against the dark sky.

The guard gestured for me to move forward, and I complied, walking slowly, my steps echoing off the cobblestones. I followed the line of sentries silently, overwhelmed by the grandeur of this place. I had no idea what lay ahead of me, and I wasn't sure I was ready to find out.

"Aw, they missed me," August muttered threateningly, his hands gliding up and down the front of his impenetrable green suit. He had adorned himself with the regal garment and a tarnished crown, the metal glinting ominously in the dim light, obscuring his piercing gaze. An ancient crest was pinned to his chest, a reminder of the power and danger that followed him.

The men in armor didn't move. They stood at attention in their emerald and silver uniforms, each one as decorated as the last. Their matching yellow sashes hung over their right shoulder, the gold-tipped spears held tightly between their fingers. They had no expression on their face at all. Not even a wrinkled forehead or a twitch in the lips.

Adonis lurched out from the shadows of the circular driveway, his aged face a map of twisted wrinkles and despair. His sunken eyes were like shadowy pits, warning us of the danger ahead. He clenched his jaw tightly and squared his hunched shoulders, trying to exude a sense of determination despite the overwhelming dread that hung so heavily in the air.

"Stick to the plan," Leo grunted. His shifty eyes scanned all of us.

"I'm still king for the next fifteen minutes, so I suggest you stop bossing me about," August clipped.

Adonis bowed dutifully as August approached, with us following close behind. A few people whispered, likely gossiping about where he had been these last few days. "Hello, sir. I trust your visit was productive."

August smirked at him. "Very."

My king clasped my hand firmly in his, sending a shiver of adrenaline racing through my veins. My heart thumped wildly within my chest, the sound of it filling my ears. Adonis stepped closer, his cobalt eyes alive with an intensity that terrified me. "Now or never," August murmured in a low, throaty whisper. It felt like I was no longer in control of my own fate—I was at their mercy. I could only hope our plan worked.

"We're right here with you, Little Monster," Atticus whispered encouragingly.

I gripped August's hand as though it were a lifeline, every muscle in my body tensed with anticipation. I marched forward, each of my footsteps seeming to reverberate. All eyes were on us; I could feel their heavy gazes like a tangible pressure against my skin. The whispers around us seemed almost deafening in the stillness, and I felt terror gripping my heart. I kept my eyes fixed on August, searching for strength in his silent reassurance. He gave my hand a gentle squeeze, curling his lips in a small smile that I tried valiantly to return.

We walked up to the steps, the guards moving their spears out of our way. Adonis stood in front of us and swung the large double doors open. Workers and members of the elite filled the space. The entire hall stood at attention, their heads bowed as we walked.

I gulped. Being back at the castle, especially after the devastating explosion, had me on edge. I felt a chill every time I heard a distant sound, as if our enemies were coming to finish us off. The knife I had concealed at my thigh offered me some comfort; I was ready to fight if the need arose. All I had to do now was declare that I had survived and forge ahead with the wedding plans with August. It didn't matter if he wasn't the rightful heir. Once our positions were solidified, we could finally end Lord Nathan's tyranny.

"Hello, everyone," August called out in a loud voice. Shocked whispers traveled through the crowd. August nodded at everyone, his eyes taking in the scene. "As you can see, my bride is alive and well."

The women around me recoiled in shock. Some even whipped out their phones to take pictures of me— the living symbol of our near-tragedy. I held my arm high, my damaged skin still exposed, raw and vulnerable. They could see it, the evidence of our attack. We'd been persecuted by Lord Nathan at our engagement party. But I wasn't scared anymore—not with Atticus and Leo at my side. They filled the air with a sense of security, a promise that I would be okay.

"Let's get this over with," Leo grumbled.

"Let's roll some heads," Atticus added, and the four of us made our way through the castle.

"How dire is the situation, Adonis?" August asked, his smile a facade. The sound of my frantic footsteps reverberated through the castle. I took quick glances around, analyzing every face that looked my way. Which ones of them were Lord Nathan's spies? Which ones were a credible threat?

"It's dire indeed, sir," Adonis replied grimly. "Lord Nathan's rumors have spread like wildfire. People are starting to doubt the legitimacy of the lords. Fear has them on edge, and they take Lord Nathan seriously, especially after the attack at your engagement party and the murders at the House of Pearl and House of Brooke."

"Lovely," August grumbled.

We strode around the bend, coming to the grand oaken doors at the end of the hall. With a creak, they slowly swung open, challenging us to enter. The room was full of seething rage, with hatred reflected in every face. Cigar smoke filled the air like a threatening fog, while whispers of dread circulated like venom.

"He *finally* shows up." A man with a dark beard and a dark expression puffed on his cigar and spoke through the cloud of smoke. He and the rest of the council stood to greet us; I noticed that no one formally bowed, though. That wasn't a good sign.

August's eyes glimmered with determination. "My deepest apologies, gentlemen. As you know, it was believed my fiancée had perished in the explosion. But it appears there was a mistake made at the hospital— she is alive! I've stayed by her side while she recuperat- ed." He swallowed hard before looking at me. "How- ever, I fear we have more obstacles to overcome. I believe it is imperative we move forward with our wedding plans."

The men's faces drained of color, and I felt their menacing gaze penetrate me. I understood their insidious ways, that they wouldn't waste a single thought on me as a woman. I knew raising my voice was futile.

But not for long.

They were ruthless. They were power-hungry.

"And you truly believe that?" The bearded man stalked toward us like a hunter. His men were following him with their hands on their weapons. He had the ferocity of a lion, with the coldheartedness to back it up. "It looks like Lady Christine. But we heard she perished in the flames." His voice was heavily tinged with suspicion and threat.

August peered at him. "The reports were wrong. Feel free to call the hospital. They'll happily explain the mix-up."

An elderly man stepped forward with trepidation. "Your Highness, forgive me for speaking out of turn, but we must discuss this dire situation. Lord Nathan's rumors have already caused a stir across the land, and it won't be long before chaos ensues! Unless we act fast to bring him down, his lies will rip apart our kingdom."

August clenched his jaw. "Right. The rumors. Rest assured I am *still* the rightful heir to the throne. I don't understand why you're allowing Lord Nathan's rumors and civil unrest to poison our kingdom. We should be focusing on bringing him down, not entertaining his foolish accusations."

He nodded, knowing his words held truth. Leo and Atticus beside me seethed with rage, and I gave them a subtle nod to show I shared their sentiment.

"Yes, Your Majesty. That is why we are gathered here," he spoke firmly. "We must act now to restore confidence in us and the House. A DNA test is the only way to prove your innocence. We must not allow doubts to linger any longer." Lord Taylor's voice echoed throughout the chamber as his gaze swept over us all. A silence settled over everyone, thick with tension and unspoken threats.

August sneered, "A DNA test? That's absurd!" His words were echoed by several others in the room. "We don't yield to terrorists!"

"But Lord Nathan's accusations are spreading," an unfamiliar voice said from the shadows in the corner. A man stepped out, and I saw a slick black ponytail and a goatee. "Your mother—may she rest in peace—is a casualty of this. We must think this through. People are beginning to lose their faith in us. If we do not take action swiftly, our kingdom will crumble to ruins. We must put this war to an end, once and for all, before more lords are killed."

"Whose side are you on, Ricardo? Are you with us or him?" a man with a round belly and thinning gray hair asked.

Ricardo stepped back and bowed his head. "I serve the king. The *rightful* king."

August crossed his arms over his chest and raised an eyebrow. "A DNA test would prove what?"

"If you are the rightful heir to the throne." The man's tone was full of venom.

Atticus cleared his throat, stealing all the attention in the room. "The only thing a DNA test would prove is that you *fear* Lord Nathan. Regardless of the outcome, it would give him leverage and power."

"Forgive me, Your Highness," a short man with blond hair said, "but this is a closed meeting. We don't need the DuPonts infiltrating this kingdom more than they already do."

August pressed his lips into a thin line. "He stays."

The tension in the room was palpable. Everyone had an opinion, and their words were beginning to reach a feverish pitch. Behind me, Leo and Atticus were standing firm, ready to support whatever decision August made.

"I think we're all overlooking something critical

here," I said, my voice shaking as I faced the intimidating stares of the powerful men before me. I knew they viewed me as insignificant, just a tool to be used in the grand scheme of things. But they had no idea what I was capable of, and I intended to show them.

"I'll endure a DuPont, but I refuse to sit here and listen to a lady who thinks her opinion matters," Lord Ricardo snapped.

My muscles tightened as I locked eyes with him. "No one is above the laws of this kingdom. Not even you. If King Augustus isn't the rightful heir, then I am. Think about what that means." My words were like a dagger, piercing through the silence of the room.

A hush fell over the room as the whispers slowly died away. All eyes were on me as I slowly nodded my head as if I had already come to the same conclusion. Everyone in this room knew that the line of ascension was a treacherous game and wanted to know where they stacked up in the hierarchy of power. "I am to marry Augustus, yes? The strongest showing of force we can make is to go through with the marriage, and it will solidify both our places as rulers. Lord Nathan is unreliable and unpredictable, and so it is reckless to allow his idle gossip to disrupt our sacred Crown's elite. We must marry and prove him wrong. We are rulers of this noble kingdom, and we will not let anyone deter us."

The older man nodded. "That's very wise, Lady Christine. The House of Rose *is* next. The sooner you marry, the less opportunities Lord Nathan has to claim her."

"Lord Nathan still objects to the marriage," another person added. "There is the question of whether or not he has a claim to her. Perhaps Lord Nathan *is* the rightful—"

"Finish that statement, and I'll have your head rolling down the streets of Aldrich," Atticus snarled. "You will not question the king."

It was hard to hear over the uproar of voices.

"Let me make this very clear." August's voice demanded everyone's attention. "I am the rightful heir. I will not have my rights taken from me because of some terrorist's groundless claims. I am marrying Lady Abernathy, and our marriage will solidify the claim that I am the rightful heir to the throne. If any of you have a problem with that, then you are welcome to raise the sword against me. Otherwise, I expect your support. I've taken the Crown, and I will not give it up. The people want leadership, and they want it now."

Silence reigned. It was like ice water pouring over their nerves. They couldn't really fight August. He was right. They were scared.

"Now, you can either side with me and put your

trust in the Crown, or you can renounce your title. Do your jobs, work together with your fellow peers, and curtail these rumors. The kingdom of Aldrich will not fall—not on my watch. We are united as one, and together we will defeat Lord Nathan. We will protect the Crown."

The tension stretched until it snapped. The men in the room clapped, shouting celebratory chants. I hadn't realized how afraid they all were. Not just of what Lord Nathan could do, but of what would happen to them if they didn't act fast enough.

As the cheers roared, one voice bellowed through the crowd, silencing them all. Lord Ricardo's eyes narrowed, his stern gaze piercing them all. "And what will you do to protect us in the meantime? We are all at risk," he growled. Everyone held their breaths, feeling a sense of foreboding and dread.

August sighed. "You will all stay here until the wedding ceremony is finished. We have enough guards and protection in place to keep you and your families safe."

An older gentleman scoffed. "You couldn't keep your own bloody engagement party safe—"

"Enough!" August roared. "You can either accept my kind generosity or take the risk. It's obvious that

Lord Nathan is working down the line. I think now that it's stopped at Lady Christine, he won't attack further."

Lord Ricardo snarled. "No. It just means she's the new target."

All eyes fell on me.

"Then she'll be heavily guarded. As will you," August said, pointing to the others.

"Lord Nathan's attacks are coordinated but sloppy." Leo cleared his throat, drawing attention to him. "My team of security experts have determined that he's enlisting poor members of the kingdom on the outskirts of town. He doesn't have the resources to take on an army."

August nodded. "Once the wedding ceremony is done, I will take my army and squash his rebellion once and for all."

"And until then?" Lord Ricardo asked.

August's expression tightened. "We must play our cards carefully. Give him no reason to believe he has any power."

Chapter Twenty-One

CHRISTINE

I was trying to focus on my book, but it wasn't easy when August's touch was so electric. His fingertips moved languidly over my flesh, sending sparks through my veins with each stroke. I gasped in response and he paused, his hands hovering just above my skin before tracing small circles around my shoulder blades.

A low sigh escaped his lips. "It's so boring in here," he grumbled. We'd been confined to his chambers for two days while the court feverishly prepared for our wedding the next morning. "We should have eloped," he added, too softly for anyone else to hear.

I twisted around to face him, my fingertips exploring the contours of his toned physique as I tried to imagine a world where I wasn't bound to the palace and its courtly rules. I was ready to marry August, but I wasn't ready to be queen. I wasn't ready to live the rest of my life in this castle.

August's gaze met mine and he brushed his thumb across my lips. This moment wasn't meant to linger, however, and he leaned in until his forehead met mine. "Let's just savor this final night before we can truly be together," he said, his voice barely above a whisper.

"Can't I go outside? I'm not a fan of seeing this," Leo said through gritted teeth.

Atticus laughed mockingly from his spot by the window. "Oh, feeling jealous? Or are you just *frustrated*? Christine can help with that, you know."

Leo's jaw clenched. "Are you being serious right now?"

"Blue balls are *very* serious," Atticus answered with amusement.

"To answer your question," August breezed, "you need to stay here. I want us all to have eyes on Christine at all times. Word about the wedding tomorrow has spread, and I don't want Lord Nathan trying anything. So pull the stick out of your ass and get over it."

Leo sighed and thrust his hands through his long hair. "Fine."

"Look at the good little soldier, obeying orders," Atticus goaded. One of these days, that DuPont was going to push Leo over the edge.

And part of me hoped I was there to see it. Experience it.

I spent more time exploring the contours of August's body, my fingertips tracing paths of fire across his flesh. I could hardly believe it was real, having such intimate access to someone so beautiful. His skin felt like silk beneath my fingertips, and shivers ran through my body as I felt the strong tendons in his neck. His hand moved lower and lower, from my side to my ribs, then finally to my hip, his touch burning me with desire.

A knock sounded at the door, and it swung open, making me flinch. A young maid walked through the threshold, curtsying awkwardly before looking up at us. She swallowed hard at the sight of all three men, her eyes traveling over each of us as she cleared her throat.

"Your Highness, Adonis and Miss Victoria have requested your presence in the dining hall," she squeaked. "They want to go over a few of your requests for tomorrow."

He waved his hand. "Tell them to do whatever. I don't care as long as I get to marry Christine."

I smiled, but the maid shifted nervously. "They insisted."

I squeezed August's hand and smiled. "You should go. It's not right to see the bride before the wedding anyway."

August straightened away from me and gave the maid a nod of acknowledgement. "Tell them I'll be right there," he said, his voice hard as steel and tinged with frustration.

The maid bowed her head once more before scurrying away. I watched her go before turning my gaze back to August. His jaw was clenched tightly and his eyes were stormy. This interruption had thrown us both off our game, leaving us to deal with an uncomfortable distance between us for the time being.

He let out a sigh as he tugged his jacket back on, adjusting the collar once more before giving me a weak smile. "I guess this is goodbye for now," he said with a hint of disappointment in his voice.

August leaned over and kissed me deeply, confident despite our audience. Perhaps there was hope for us yet. Or he was just in a good mood because he knew we'd be married tomorrow and he'd have me forever. "I'd rather spend all night with you," he whispered over my lips.

"August!" I giggled. "We don't get to stick to all of

our traditions, but I'd like this one. I want to surprise you with my dress."

He let out a lengthy sigh. The dress I'd picked out was last minute but still gorgeous. I couldn't wait to walk down the aisle to him in it. "Fine," he relented. "But you don't leave Leo's or Atticus's sight," he said against my lips.

"Oh," Atticus interjected. "We won't even leave this room."

August gave him a wry look, absorbing the insinuations in his tone with a frown. "Tomorrow is the big day. You'll take my last name. Wear my ring. Say your vows to *me*." Though he was speaking to me, I had a feeling that his words were meant for the other men in this room.

"Yes, yes. You've staked your claim. Go see what it is Adonis wants," I giggled.

The moment he was gone, Atticus got out of his chair and walked over to the bed.

"I've been eagerly awaiting this all day," he growled, gripping me tight and lifting me up from the mattress. The inviting aroma of sandalwood and leather hit my senses, and I sunk into his embrace, pressing my lips to his. I felt his ragged breath on my skin, and the sensation ignited a flame deep within me.

He kissed me hungrily, his fingers dancing through

my hair as his body drew ever closer. Leo watched intently, his heat-filled gaze radiating desire.

I pulled away, searching Atticus's face. "What are you doing?" I breathed.

"Tomorrow you'll be in his bed, but tonight I need you in mine," he said in a husky voice, gripping my face and forcing me to meet his gaze. His eyes burned with a primal fire as he slowly spoke, "And you know what else, Little Monster? I'm the one that's gonna walk you down the aisle."

I would have laughed, but the seriousness in his tone made me stop. "You are?"

"Yes. Because I own you. He's just letting you borrow his name. I won't be giving you away, Little Monster."

He smothered my lips with an intense, passionate kiss. His grip tightened, becoming almost predatory. I could feel the caged anger and jealousy radiating off of him. I broke away reluctantly, giving him the sternest look that I could muster.

"Atticus," I croaked, my throat dry with desire. "Stop…take it slow."

"Never," he whispered before reaching under my shirt and tracing my soft skin with his fingers. "It's hard to go slow when you look so delicious and fuckable, Little Monster."

Leo watched us hungrily, his pupils dilated in anticipation. My breath quickened as Atticus's lips brushed my own. His hands moved to my hips, and he looked me deep in the eyes, his voice rumbling with a sexy growl.

"Oh, Little Monster. You want him too? I'll share if you're a good girl."

I felt my heart flutter as Leo's hot gaze branded me. Atticus roughly ripped my shirt off, sending shivers through my spine, and I felt the snap of my bra as it broke and fell to the ground. I was completely exposed.

"And you know what, Little Monster? I'm going to make you mine," he purred into my ear, a teasing smile playing on his lips. "I'm going to make you so wet that he'll just slide right inside you. Is that what you want?"

He kissed my neck, and I felt a shudder run through me as his fingers teased my nipples. He whispered more dirty promises in between kisses, coaxing me closer to an edge I could no longer deny.

"Okay." I was powerless to stop him. He'd made it clear that he wasn't going to take no for an answer.

"And tomorrow, when you walk down the aisle? You're going to have our cum dripping down your legs."

"I refuse," Leo protested, though he sounded forced.

Luckily, I wasn't distracted by his rejection.

"Let me do this for you," Atticus murmured against my neck.

He forced me to my knees. I immediately knew what he was going to do. He reached into his pants and pulled out his cock, already dripping with pre-cum.

"I don't want your mouth," he grunted. "I want your pussy. You're going to be a good girl and bend over the bed. I'm going to get this pretty little fuck hole nice and wet for us." He pumped the head of his cock against my lips. "I just wanted to see you kneeling before me for a moment."

"You're seriously going to make me watch this?" Leo gritted out, his voice harsh and uneven.

Atticus's gaze smoldered with lust. "Look at you, I can see it in your eyes. Are you just going to sit there and watch, or are you gonna give in to temptation and show me what you can do?"

Leo's mouth snapped shut and he stared at the floor.

"Oh, Little Monster," Atticus chuckled. He held his hand out for me and helped me stand. Then, he spun me around and pressed on my back until I was bent over on the mattress, with my ass in the air. "Now, I want you to spread your legs for me. Show us both how pretty and pink you are."

I swallowed hard, struggling to focus on anything other than Atticus's hands on my body as he trailed them over my skin.

"Do you want it?" he murmured, his wicked fingers trailing down my spine. "Tell me, Little Monster. I'll make him fuck you until you scream his name." His lips against my ear, I could feel his possessive, jealous energy radiating from his body. I shivered, trying to draw strength from the promise of pleasure in his voice and not the feral jealousy burning in Leo's eyes as he watched us.

"Please," I whispered.

"Say it," he murmured, sliding his fingers between my folds. "And I'll make him fuck you. I'll bend you over your wedding dress and make you tell him how you want his hard cock inside of you."

The words were spoken in a low voice, but the pleasure he gave me made my hips buck. I opened my eyes to see him staring at me. "I...I want all of that."

"Such a good girl," he crooned. "Come here, Leo."

"No," he rasped.

"Don't make me hold you at gunpoint again," Atticus argued. "You know you want to. You know you're dying to feel how good her tight little pussy feels. If you're scared, we can do it together. Wouldn't you like that, Little Monster? Both of us filling your tight hole with our cocks at the same time?"

Fuck, his words were going to ruin me. I'd never imagined doing something like that, but now that Atticus had put the visual in my mind, I couldn't stop thinking about it.

"Put a finger inside of her," Atticus told him. "Watch how good she feels. Then, if you still want to hold back, we'll stop."

I tried to look at Leo again, but he was still staring at the floor. His body slowly relaxed and he shook his head slowly. When Atticus brushed my hair behind my ear, I turned my face to him. He kissed my cheek gently and gave me a wink.

"This is your last chance, Leo. Don't make me ask again."

I felt the anticipation rise within me as he yet again remained silent. His refusal was maddening, and I clenched my fists, frustration coursing through me.

But before I could speak, I felt Leo's hands on my waist, and his hard body pressed against my back.

He leaned in and whispered in my ear, his breath hot against my neck. "Just this once," he growled, brushing his lips against my cheek. "I have to have you at least once."

I arched my back, allowing him to pull me closer against him. His hands explored every inch of me until I moaned in pleasure, calling out his name. And then, he sunk his finger inside of me and thrust.

His fingers moved faster and faster, cleanly breaking through any lingering denial he may have had.

"That's very good," Atticus whispered. "I knew you couldn't hold back. You've been *dying* to feel her. You just needed someone to give you permission."

Leo slowly slid another finger inside, groaning as he did. "She's so tight. I want to feel her squeeze my cock," Leo growled.

"You could be inside of her right now. All you have to do is ask."

Leo groaned and bit my ass cheek. "You're making it hard to concentrate."

"Such a bad boy," Atticus said, his voice breathless. He leaned over me and licked my neck. "You've been hiding in the shadows for so long. Why don't you take control, Leo?"

Leo groaned again, his fingers moving faster.

"You can come inside of her," Atticus told him. "You can fill her little pussy up. All you have to do is ask." Atticus's filthy talk and Leo's movements were making me writhe. "Yes, Little Monster," he murmured.

Atticus shifted, then quickly reached between Leo's legs. We all froze as Atticus sunk under the waistband of his pants and wrapped his fingers around his shaft. "Let's get him nice and hard. Make him want you so bad he can't hold back."

"Stop," Leo grunted.

"Why on earth would I do that?" Atticus replied while pumping him. "Don't mistake this for anything but pleasure. You're nothing more than a tool to make my Little Monster feel good." Atticus removed his hand, then unbuttoned Leo's pants before shoving them down in one swift move.

Leo and I both were breathing so hard I couldn't think straight. Atticus worked his cock, stroking him with the familiarity only a man could have. I was transfixed by the sight, by the raw masculinity and lust.

I moaned as Leo's fingers moved faster, plunging in and out of me. His other hand reached around to play with my clit. I could feel my orgasm approaching. I whimpered as he moved his fingers faster and faster, his hips pumping against my backside.

"What does she taste like?" Leo's voice was husky but clear.

"Why don't you see for yourself?" Atticus said.

I gasped when Leo's fingers left me. I continued to

look over my shoulder with wide eyes as he slowly licked each finger, savoring the taste of me as Atticus ran his hands down Leo's cock. Every part of my skin that was exposed to the air tingled, from my neck to the small of my back.

"Is this what you wanted?" Atticus asked us both.

"Yes." Leo's voice was even softer than usual. Atticus dropped to his knees and bumped his lips against Leo's cock. Teasing him. Taunting him.

"Yes," I replied. I wanted to see Atticus wrap his lips around Leo.

But he didn't. "I won't suck you off, Leo, though I can tell you're aching for it. Why don't you make my girl feel good, hmm?"

Leo released my hip and pressed his face between my legs, fucking me with his tongue. He was quick and demanding, as if he'd just jumped off the edge of a cliff and was free falling into hell. The feeling was so intense that I arched my back, releasing a scream of pleasure.

"Yes!" Atticus groaned before standing up. He pulled Leo's head back and hovered his lips over his. "You better taste that pussy. You better drink down every damn drop." Atticus released Leo, then started tearing off his own clothes.

A moment later, he was standing in front of us, his

cock hard and in need. His gaze burned into Leo, waiting for his next move.

Leo ran his tongue up and down my slit, collecting every drop of my arousal. When he reached my clit, I whimpered and rolled over. As I moved up the mattress, Leo crawled after me, chasing the high of my pleasure with his mouth.

"Fuck, you taste good," he rasped, his voice breaking with need.

"Of course she does." Atticus grunted while climbing onto the bed beside us.

"I…" My words faded, drowning in pleasure.

"How's my Little Monster doing?" Atticus asked me as he settled beside me. I had two naked, hard, feral men on my bed.

"Unbelievable," I whispered.

Atticus reached over me and grabbed two pillows. He separated them and laid them on the bed. "When Leo's done eating that pussy, I'm going to make you ride both of our cocks."

My stomach flipped, and I struggled to catch my breath. In that moment, I didn't know if I'd ever been so turned on. The idea of both of them fucking me made my body buzz.

Atticus grabbed my hips and pulled me back onto his lap. I was facing Leo with my hips straddling Atticus. Leo bent over to once again place his tongue on my clit before Atticus thrust into me. I cried out and arched my back as he grabbed my hair and pulled my head back. Leo's tongue continued to work its magic as Atticus rocked into me, moving his cock in and out.

I whined and lost my breath as Atticus slammed into me. The combination of Leo's tongue and Atticus's cock was too much for my body. I couldn't think, I couldn't breathe. All I could do was feel the electricity pulsating through my body, a constant reminder of the pleasure that was taking over me.

"God, Little Monster, you're so fucking tight. How do you feel?"

"I don't know. I'm so close. I feel like I'm going to…" I couldn't finish my sentence, the words dying on my lips.

"Let go. Come on my dick."

My body tensed and I cried out as the orgasm crashed into my body, sending tingling sensations throughout every inch of me. Leo licked like his fucking life depended on it, sucking my clit, wringing out every inch of pleasure.

"Stop licking her and get your cock ready."

Leo paused and sat up. I watched while Atticus thrust in and out as Leo ran his hand over his shaft, watching with heavy eyes.

"Now, Leo," I begged.

Atticus leaned me back, my thighs resting on his strong arms. Leo's eyes locked with mine as he pressed against my entrance, causing me to gasp with anticipation. "She's so tight," he muttered before pushing himself further at my entrance, right where Atticus was already spearing me, his breathing turning ragged as he filled me up. I let out a scream of pleasure as Leo thrust into me. I felt like I was the only one in the world, Leo's gaze never leaving mine and Atticus whispering sexy words in my ear. My body was ablaze with their touches, and I felt completely overwhelmed.

"Yes!" I screamed as Leo filled my body. I was so full I couldn't breathe. I looked over my shoulder and met Atticus's heavy gaze.

"You feel so fucking good," Leo gritted out, his voice hoarse. "This…is different but—".

"So good," Atticus said before biting my shoulder.

"Oh, God," I moaned. I looked down to see both of their cocks buried deep inside my pussy while Atticus still rocked in and out. Leo moved his hips, pushing a little deeper every time. He held my hip tight as he moved in and out, a slow rhythm to match his thrusts.

"Is it good?" Atticus asked. I turned my head to see his teeth clenched and his face tight with the exertion of holding back.

"Yes." I nodded while writhing on top of him, wanting to feel more.

"Oh fuck," Atticus whispered, his breath hitching.

Leo moaned as he pushed his cock into my tight entrance, the both of them filling me until I had no room left to breathe. Both of them were so big, so powerful. A rush of pleasure coursed through me, making me push my hips back to take more of Leo.

"Like that, Little Monster?" Atticus asked in my ear. He pulled back before ramming into me with all the force he could muster. He held his hand against my throat, keeping me from moving upward. "Do you like that? Do you like taking more of us?"

I whimpered, unable to speak as Atticus and Leo started pumping into me again, making me yell and scream in pleasure. Both of them moved with perfect synchronization.

"That's it," Atticus murmured. "Take more of us. I can feel Leo's cock. He's close, Little Monster." Both of their breaths were ragged and heavy.

I cried out and closed my eyes as every bit of my body buzzed. Leo pushed into me, his cock pressing against Atticus's. A burst of pleasure crashed through me at the new sensation.

A rush of bliss spread through my veins. The orgasm was raw and tangible. It was so intense, so wild, that I clenched my jaw and squeezed my eyes shut.

"Look at me," Atticus commanded.

I opened my eyes and turned once more to meet his gaze. His face was set and hard, his eyes red. He had been fighting his release for so long it took everything he had to give me that order.

Leo pressed into me more and more, fucking me with Atticus. I cried out and gripped onto his shoulders for support.

"Fuck," Leo grunted.

"Fuck. Yes," Atticus hissed.

"Come one more time, Little Monster," Atticus whispered in my ear, his lips against my skin.

I stifled my scream as we moved together. Atticus's hands were under my thighs, pulling me back into him while Leo pounded into me from above.

Leo grunted as both cocks surged in and out of me. Atticus lifted up with his legs, forcing me to bounce on both of their cocks. "Look at her." Leo's voice was husky, his eyes locked on Atticus's cock fucking me. "Look at how fucking perfect she is. How tight."

My vision blurred, and I couldn't even breathe.

"Come," Atticus ordered. "Let go, Little Monster."

I held my breath as my orgasm approached. I could

hear both of their breathing, feel their movements deep inside of me.

Leo encouraged me, too. "Come now, baby!"

My body jerked as I screamed, my orgasm slamming into me. It was intense, shattering, and soul destroying. My body tingled, I felt like I was on fire. My skin turned to goose bumps, my body quivered. It was unlike anything I'd ever experienced before.

My orgasm continued, Leo's and Atticus's cocks deep inside of me. Everything around me faded, the room disappeared. It was just Atticus and Leo fucking me, making me feel good. I wasn't alone. I wasn't lost.

When I finally looked at Leo, he was staring down at my pussy, watching his and Atticus's cock disappear inside of me. He dropped his head and closed his eyes as he thrust into me. When he opened his lids again, his eyes were focused on me.

"Damn, you're so beautiful," he murmured. He leaned forward and kissed me. I could taste my arousal on his lips. "Shit," he moaned into the kiss before releasing my lips. "I'm going to come."

"Me, too," Atticus grunted.

I was still high on my own orgasm but reached out and squeezed his thigh. "Fill me up." I held his gaze as he fucked me, and I watched as he came.

The arms holding me up collapsed, and I fell back.

I was now lying on Atticus's chest. Leo went limp on top of me. I looked over my shoulder to see Leo's hand clasped in Atticus's hand. They were both breathing hard.

We lay like that for a few minutes, completely spent, completely relaxed. I couldn't help but finally feel like I had them all.

Now, I just had to keep them.

Chapter Twenty-Two

CHRISTINE

A sharp, jarring sound ripped me from my sleep. I jolted to see Atticus violently yanked from our bed and hurled to the ground. Leo's muscles quivered and bulged as he stood, fists raised and ready to fight. The masked assailant lunged for me, and I felt his slimy hands grasp my ankle as I tumbled toward the mattress face-first. Suddenly, Leo's voice thundered, "Run, Christine!" Adrenaline surged through me and I scrambled from the bed, intent on escape. But the masked man was relentless, a grip like steel clamped onto my ankle. I whirled around and slammed my fist into his throat with all my strength, eliciting a gargled scream as he crumpled to the floor.

A deafening silence filled the room, only to be broken by the powerful grunts of Atticus as he fought against the towering silhouette of a man. The man had broad shoulders and was like an unmovable wall.

I screamed out in fear, my voice echoing through the chamber, "Atticus!" But the man on the ground had reached out to grab my ankle. No matter how hard I kicked, I could not escape his grasp. He dragged me back down with a strength that felt unnatural.

The masked man's gruff voice boomed through the room. "Watch that one!" he barked. "Boss said she's a skilled fighter." His steel grip on my arm jerked me back, and I fought against his strength. I tried to wriggle away, but the cold edge of a blade pressed into my neck, reminding me of my fragility. I dared a glance at Leo, whose eyes were ablaze with terror and despair.

The man had no idea what he was up against. I took a deep breath to steel my heart against what would come. Inhale. Exhale. Inhale. Exhale. I was ready to fight. With a guttural roar, I launched myself at him with all the strength that I had.

I was an unstoppable force. This was what I had trained so hard for.

I surged forward, snatching the dagger from his grip. I felt the sting as my skin split open and the warm trickle of blood ran down my arm. With a fierce grunt,

I swung my fist into his nose. There was a sickening crack as his face crumbled beneath my knuckles. My enemy tumbled to the ground, clutching his broken nose as his eyes widened in fear.

My heart pounded with exhilaration. I felt invincible. I was going to save everyone.

Leo hit another masked man while Atticus rolled on the ground, fighting for his life.

I jumped out of bed, ready to kill anyone who came close to me. The man on the ground with a broken nose grabbed my leg, but I stomped on his face, bringing him down as I released a scream of fury.

This was war.

This was my life.

I wasn't going to let anyone take me or the men I loved.

Time seemed to stand still as I moved in slow motion, my leg arching and pointed toes thrusting forward in a blink, connecting with the man's abdomen. Then a sudden burst of strength surged through my veins as I grabbed his knife from the floor and plunged it deep into his neck. Hot blood sprayed onto my face, and as I wiped it away with a triumphant grin, I felt a rush of adrenaline like never before. It was me or him; and I was determined to live.

The masked man's blood was hot on my hand, the

heat pulsing from it. It turned cold as it smeared down my arm, and I opened my mouth to inhale. My tongue was like a snake, flicking out to catch a drop of crimson death. Salty, metallic. Like the taste when you bite your tongue.

I turned and watched Atticus get hammered by a masked man twice his size.

"Atticus!" I screamed as I pulled the knife out of my victim's neck and thrust it toward his attacker. The blade sunk into his back, and he released Atticus with a groan.

"Stupid fucking bitch!" he roared before spinning to attack me.

I ducked to avoid his thunderous punch, but he was too fast. His fist crashed against my face, sending my head spinning and stars bursting in my vision. My words were stuck in a jumbled mess as I screamed, "Leo! Atticus! Get out of here!" But before I could do anything else, I felt my body sliding down the wall and my jaw start to throb. I saw Atticus attempt to fight back, but the man was too powerful. The assailant threw him off with ease, and Atticus landed with a thud on the ground, his pale chest heaving in terror. Blood poured from a deep gash in his head, and I felt a wave of despair wash over me.

A loud roar filled the air, making my head jerk up.

Leo thundered toward us, leaving a collection of bodies on the ground. He'd stolen a knife from one of them and slammed it into the man's neck. Through the mask, I could see our attacker's eyes bulge in their sockets from the pain.

Atticus pulled himself off the ground with a grunt. "We have to run."

"We have to save August," I said. Leo tossed me a robe as he pulled pants over his boxers. Atticus found his button-up shirt and thrust his arms through the sleeves.

"My priority is getting you out of here. We have to go," he growled.

I wasn't listening. August was somewhere inside and we had to save him.

Leo twirled the knife in his hand and nodded once. Blood coated his exposed skin, and there was a deep cut on his lip. "Let's hurry up."

We rushed down the hallway, Atticus at my back and Leo at the head. The only light was from flickering candles, which cast sinister shadows across the walls. The walls reverberated with the roars of our enemies and anguished screams. My heart pounded with fear and anticipation as we ran, desperate to reach safety before it was too late.

"What's happening out there?" Leo asked.

The walls quaked as the sounds of combat echoed through the corridor. Atticus grabbed my shoulder firmly, his eyes full of fear. "War. All hell is breaking loose. They've taken everyone." I shuddered, turning my gaze to the windows that had been blasted to pieces. Shards of glass littered the ground, a reminder of what was to come. The hallway felt like a deathtrap, a winding tunnel of gray with no escape in sight. I could feel a sense of dread and desperation clogging my throat. This was it—we were going to fight for our lives.

The hallway ended at a set of double doors, and we all halted, unsure of what waited on the other side. The scent of blood, sweat, and death filled the hall. "We have to get out of here," Leo growled. "This is the only way."

"Let's fucking do this!" Atticus flung the doors open and we stepped into the chaos. The main hall was engulfed in flames, a violent battle waging between two factions. Everywhere I looked, there were flashes of gunfire and screeches of pain. Bodies were strewn across the castle, some unmoving while others screamed out in agony. I could see desperation in the eyes of the defenders, their faces twisted with fear or rage as they fought against their attackers. Atticus grabbed my arm, his grip tightening around me as if to protect me from the slaughter that surrounded us.

I stepped over a dead lord who was bleeding out on the tile as another man wearing all black started sprinting toward us. Leo intercepted him and landed a punch in his stomach. Bullets soared by my head as Atticus tackled another masked man. I found a discarded gun on the floor and quickly picked it up. When I saw another attacker heading straight toward the double doors we had just walked through, I raised my gun, cocking it with my thumb. I held my breath, aimed, and pulled the trigger. The bullet hit the man in the shoulder, but he managed to keep himself steady. Another bullet whizzed past me, and I spun around, but no one was there. "Leo! Atticus! Are you okay?" I screamed as I turned back around to find them fighting for their lives.

"Christine!" Atticus scrambled to his feet, holding a limp Leo in his arms. "He's hurt!" Atticus glanced around, fear in his eyes. "Find a way out of here, or we're going to die."

I swallowed the lump in my throat. "Leave me," Leo gurgled. There was a wound pouring blood in his gut.

I moved to help Atticus, but someone grabbed my arm, dragging me toward the large double doors. "No!" Leo's voice was unrecognizable, his eyes wild.

A man wearing all black tackled Leo and Atticus to

the ground, and I aimed the gun at the man dragging me. He was nearly as tall as Atticus, but I'd been trained to fight men twice my size.

I pulled the trigger, but no bullet lodged in his skull.

Fuck. No more ammunition. Rearing back, I slammed the gun against his temple. There was no way I'd go down without a fight.

"Bitch!" he growled as I punched him again and again. I gathered my energy and kicked him as hard as I could. He fell to the ground and my fists flew, hitting him in the face and chest. My hands were bloody and my knuckles were raw, but I kept going. I kept fighting.

Blood poured from my lip, nose, and jaw as I rammed my knee into his groin. He gasped in pain, but before I could hit him again, he threw me over his shoulder, spinning me around until I was face-first on the hard floor. "The boss said to keep you alive, but I think it'll be much more fun to kill you."

I got to my knees and he grabbed my neck. "Let her go," Atticus growled. He was bleeding profusely from his head.

The man's breath was hot on my face as he leaned in, his fingers slowly tightening around my throat. "You dumb cunt," he hissed. I could feel my airways constricting as my vision slowly started to fade. Tears stung my eyes. I was going to die right here in this castle, surrounded by hundreds of forgotten souls, never to be seen again.

Rage and desperation surged through me. I had to survive. I thrashed and kicked, screaming as loud as I could in a vain attempt to draw help, but it was too late. I felt my strength waning, and the darkness closing in around me…

A bullet traveled through the room and landed right between his eyes. He fell forward on top of me, crushing me under the weight of his body.

A thunderous boom echoed through the grand hall, followed by a myriad of soldiers falling to their knees. Atticus gasped for breath, his panic palpable. I trembled as a figure emerged from the commotion, gun in hand and locked onto his target. Theodore DuPont strode forward with a menacing ferocity, his eyes cold and unforgiving. His booming voice filled the room. "I told you not to kill her! Can't anyone follow directions?" As I looked into the hard gaze of DuPont, I felt pure terror in my bones and knew that this man betrayed us.

I shoved the dead man off of me and pulled myself up as Atticus and Leo groaned on the floor. "What's going on?" I asked in a shaky voice. Soldiers fell to their knees and bowed, not wanting to give up their life.

My fingers closed around the blade, my heart pounding in my chest at the sight of it. A lifeline.

"Father," Atticus gasped, shock and disbelief etched on his face. "What is the meaning of this?"

Theodore DuPont sneered, his eyes gleaming with malicious intent. "I'm aligning myself with an ally that knows what it takes to get the job done."

Fury coursed through me—I knew we couldn't trust him! I lunged forward, brandishing the weapon, ready for a fight. He clicked his tongue mockingly and stepped back. "I'll kill you," I vowed through gritted teeth, fear and determination pumping through my veins.

"No," he said, his voice dark and deep. "You won't." He nodded toward a man while rolling his neck. "Bring out the prisoner."

I trembled as two men dragged August's limp body along the bloody floor. My breath caught in my throat as they dropped him on the ground, one of them kicking him in the ribs as he lay there. I took another step. "August!"

Theodore scoffed. His voice dripped with hatred. "I know my son taught you to be a killing machine. You can try attacking me if you want, yet Augustus will be a lifeless corpse before you even take a single step." Another masked man cocked his gun and pressed it to August's temple. "Love is a feeble emotion. And it will take you down, Lady Christine."

I swallowed. "What do you want from me?"

His face broke out in a wide grin. "I want you to marry Lord Nathan."

"No!" Atticus screamed. The two men holding him back struggled to keep him still. Theodore glared at his son, disgusted by his actions.

"Or what?" I asked.

Theodore DuPont's burning eyes bore into mine. "Or I'll kill everyone you love. Lord Nathan will be the next king. And I'll be his business partner." He paused to address Atticus. "We're only as strong as our alliances, Atticus. It's time for a new reign."

I shook my head. "I can't."

"Why?" he asked with a boisterous, evil laugh. "Is it because you *love* Augustus? Because you *love* my son? You're nothing but a whore. You don't know what love is. It's a weakness. It's a weakness that plays you. It's a weakness I own."

Oh God. He was truly evil. "Fuck you," I spat.

"Marry him or I'll kill them."

"You'd kill your own son?" I choked out. "Why can't I marry Atticus?"

Atticus screamed as the two men holding him down pressed a gun to his temple. Theodore's eyes turned dark. "I'd kill anyone not strong enough to lead. And you can't marry Atticus because you aren't good enough for him. You're just like Isabelle." He frowned, as if her memory angered him. "I needed Lord Nathan's army, and he needs your hand in marriage. This is nothing more than a business transaction, and you'll be the person to pay."

"Christine," Atticus pleaded. "Don't give in."

"No," I said.

"Kill them," he snapped.

The man hovering over August pulled back the safety on his gun, the clicking sound ricocheting against my skull.

I took another step forward. "No." I shook my head, tears streaming down my cheeks. "Please don't hurt them."

Theodore DuPont clenched and unclenched his jaw. "Then marry Lord Nathan."

"Fine," I whispered.

"What?" Atticus's eyes burned through the tears. "Christine, no."

"You can't marry Lord Nathan," Leo moaned.

"I have no choice." I slumped in defeat, my heart shattering into a million pieces.

"I will kill you!" Atticus roared at his father. "I will kill you!"

I dropped the knife in my hand, seemingly having no choice. "Fine," I whispered, making Leo and Atticus scream in protest. August's finger twitched. "I'll do what you ask." I swiped away the tears and soaked in the horror around me. Leo's moans and Atticus's pleas faded into the background. I couldn't think about them. I couldn't think about their pain. Everyone was staring at me. They were waiting for me to decide everything. I had the power in my hands and the weight of their lives on my shoulders.

"Don't do it, Christine," Leo wheezed. "Let me die."

I looked at Leo and Atticus. Atticus was holding his ear, blood flowing from between his fingers. Leo was clutching his stomach and sweating like crazy. I couldn't do that to either of them.

"No," I whispered. Theodore snapped his fingers. Two men grabbed my arms and held me still. Their hot breath feathered over my skin. "If you hurt any of them, I'll ruin you," I promised. Theodore DuPont would die a slow, painful death.

Theodore walked over to me, a gleam in his eye. "I'd like to see you try," he said before grabbing my chin.

My body ached; every joint felt as if it had been shattered. Sweat poured down my forehead as a fever raged through my veins. The doctor plucked the bullet from my abdomen and stitched me up, but I could feel the infection gradually taking over. I only had a limited time before the pain consumed me entirely.

Atticus paced around the cold stone cell, his face a mask of fury. He held himself responsible for our current plight, and I couldn't blame him for it. His father was the one that betrayed us. His father was working with Lord Nathan to steal away Christine and make her marry someone else. Just as I had finally won her heart, she was torn away from me again. I had been cursed ever since I laid eyes on Christine.

I knew what I had to do: break free and stop his father's insane plan.

I wrenched myself upright, fighting past the searing agony crawling up my ribs and the onslaught of dizziness that threatened to drag me down. It was no surprise that this had happened. I was dying. If I couldn't acquire the antibiotics to save me, I knew I'd become another faceless tragedy in this political battle for power, consumed by my own guilt and sorrow.

And then her fate was sealed, for it would be another man that she'd marry, not me. My heart sank and my lungs grew shallow, as if I had no more breath to take. The pain that overwhelmed me felt like it had no bounds, as if I was a prisoner of my own despair. All the guilt and sadness I felt swirled around me like an unending tornado of agony, leaving me feeling so intensely lost and broken.

I'd been down in the dungeon plenty of times as a guard, but never as a prisoner. The cramped, dark space was barely lit by a flickering torch on the wall, its dim light casting eerie shadows about the rough stone walls and damp, blackened floor. Every time I inhaled, I was sucker punched with the musky scent of decay and raw sewage.

Atticus watched me, worried. "Sit down and rest,"

he growled. "You're no use to us dead." He had a dark bruise on his jaw, and his clothes were covered in splatters of blood.

"I don't want to sit here and do nothing."

Atticus clenched his fists. "Me neither, but we don't have much of a choice. And you definitely aren't in any condition to pretend to be the hero, Leo."

I was the useless one in this dynamic.

I was the poor man.

I was the one without power or influence.

For the good of the mission, for the good of the team, for the good of Christine, it would be better if I just gave up.

I failed her. I failed everyone.

I would have to let her go.

She deserved better.

She deserved the kind of life she would have with Augustus and Atticus.

"How long before the wedding?" Augustus asked. He was sulking in a corner of our cell. We all felt hopeless, but he seemed to be the most defeated. Atticus was angry. Augustus was devastated.

I was dying.

"I'm not sure," I mumbled.

"My father won't want to waste time," Atticus

replied. It was probably uncomfortable for him to not be in control of a situation.

I let out a groan as a wave of dizziness washed over me. Augustus scooted closer and touched my forehead with the back of his hand. "Shit, he's feverish. It's not good," he said while peering at me with concerned eyes. I didn't think I'd ever had him look at me with anything but indifference.

"They won't let him die," Atticus said, though he didn't sound convinced.

Augustus shook his head. "I don't know…"

I could feel my pulse throbbing painfully in my neck, as if my heart had been squeezed by some unseen force, threatening to burst at any moment. The metallic tang of blood filled my mouth, and I swallowed hard, looking up at my friends and feeling the darkness closing in around me.

"They won't…" I murmured, my eyes fluttering.

"Leo," Atticus's voice sounded from some faraway place, far from the suffocating cell. "Hold on, man."

I tried to murmur something else but couldn't quite understand what I said. I felt my heart falter, and I gasped with the pain that coursed through my body, burning me to the core.

"Shh, it's alright, buddy, we're here." I heard Augustus's voice ring out and felt his hand on my shoulder. I gripped it tight and he squeezed in return.

The last person I thought about was Christine. I wondered if I'd still be her shadow in death.

The Crown Times

Lord Nathan and Lady Abernathy Announce Engagement!

Acknowledgments

It is with sincere gratitude that I recognize all those that helped me bring this story to life.

Helayna Trask

Amanda Anderson

Katie Friend

Lauren Campbell

Rita Rees

Claire Jones

Meggan Cook

As always, a heartfelt thank you to my family for their unending support. I'd also like to thank Quincy Mayes, for being my fantastic assistant and friend. Special thanks to Heather Maher and Amanda Avendano for letting me read the first chapter of this book to them at Book Bonanza. Their excitement and encouragement pushed me to continue. And lastly, thank you to Brittany Franks and Christine Estevez, who work hard to get my books out in the world.

About the Author

Coralee June is an *USA Today* bestselling romance writer who enjoys engaging projects and developing real, raw, and relatable characters. She is an English major from Texas State University and has had an intense interest in literature since her youth. She currently resides with her husband and three children in Dallas, Texas, where she enjoys long walks through the ice-cream aisle at her local grocery store.

WWW.AUTHORCORALEEJUNE.COM

@authorcoraleejune

www.ingramcontent.com/pod-product-compliance
Lightning Source LLC
Chambersburg PA
CBHW021213310726
48971CB00006B/1550